WAR AND PEACE

BOOK FIVE : 1806-07

By Leo Tolstoy

War and Peace Book 5
by Leo Tolstoy

ISBN: 978-93-94973-57-2

Published by

DOUBLE 9 BOOKS

2/13-B, Ansari Road
Daryaganj, New Delhi - 110002
info@double9books.com
www.double9books.com
Tel. 011-40042856

Printed in India.

About the Author

Leo Tolstoy was a Russian creator known for his books War and Peace which is viewed as the best book of pragmatist fiction. Tolstoy is additionally viewed as world's best author by quite a few people. Additionally an ethical scholar and a social reformer, Tolstoy had extreme moralistic points of view. In later life, he turned into an intense Christian rebel and anarcho-conservative.

Leo Tolstoy Born in Yasnaya Polyana on September 9, 1828, He had a place with a notable honorable Russian family. He was the fourth among five offspring of Count Nikolai Ilyich Tolstoy and Countess Mariya Tolstaya, both of whom kicked the bucket passing on their youngsters to be raised by family members.

In 1844, Tolstoy was acknowledged into Kazan University. Incapable to graduate past the subsequent year, Tolstoy got back to Yasnava Polyana and afterward invested energy going among Moscow and St. Petersburg. With some functioning information on a few dialects, he turned into a multilingual. Yet again the recently observed youth pulled in Tolstoy towards drinking, visiting massage parlors and most betting which left him in weighty obligation and anguish however Tolstoy before long acknowledged he was carrying on with a brutish life and endeavored college tests with the expectation that he would acquire a situation with the public authority, yet finished yet up in Caucuses serving in the military continuing in the strides of his senior sibling.

In Year 1862, Leo Tolstoy wedded Sophia Andreevna Behrs, generally called Sonya, who was 16 years more youthful than him. The couple had thirteen youngsters, of which, five passed on at an early age. Sonya went about as Tolstoy's secretary, editor and monetary chief while he made two out of his most prominent works. Their initial wedded life was loaded up with happiness.

He started composing his show-stopper, War and Peace in 1862. The six volumes of the work were distributed somewhere in the range of 1863 and 1869. With 580 characters got from history and others made by Tolstoy, this extraordinary novel takes on investigating the hypothesis of history and the irrelevance of noted figures like Alexander and Napoleon. Anna Karenina, Tolstoy's next epic was begun in 1873 and distributed totally in 1878.

Contents

BOOK FIVE : 1806-07

CHAPTER I

A fter his interview with his wife Pierre left for Petersburg. At the Torzhók post station, either there were no horses or the postmaster would not supply them. Pierre was obliged to wait. Without undressing, he lay down on the leather sofa in front of a round table, put his big feet in their overboots on the table, and began to reflect.

"Will you have the portmanteaus brought in? And a bed got ready, and tea?" asked his valet.

Pierre gave no answer, for he neither heard nor saw anything. He had begun to think of the last station and was still pondering on the same question—one so important that he took no notice of what went on around him. Not only was he indifferent as to whether he got to Petersburg earlier or later, or whether he secured accommodation at this station, but compared to the thoughts that now occupied him it was a matter of indifference whether he remained there for a few hours or for the rest of his life.

The postmaster, his wife, the valet, and a peasant woman selling Torzhók embroidery came into the room offering their services. Without changing his careless attitude, Pierre looked at them over his spectacles unable to understand what they wanted or how they could go on living without having solved the problems that so absorbed him. He had been engrossed by the same thoughts ever since the day he returned from Sokólniki after the duel and had spent that first agonizing, sleepless night. But now, in the solitude of the journey, they seized him with special force. No matter what he thought about, he always returned to these same questions which he could not solve and yet could not cease to ask himself. It was as if the thread of the chief screw which held his life together were stripped, so that the screw could not get in or out, but went on turning uselessly in the same place.

The postmaster came in and began obsequiously to beg his excellency to wait only two hours, when, come what might, he would let his excellency have the courier horses. It was plain that he was lying and only wanted to get more money from the traveler.

"Is this good or bad?" Pierre asked himself. "It is good for me, bad for another traveler, and for himself it's unavoidable, because he needs money for food; the man said an officer had once given him a thrashing for letting a private traveler have the courier horses. But the officer thrashed him because he had to get on as quickly as possible. And I," continued Pierre, "shot Dólokhov because I considered myself injured, and Louis XVI was executed because they considered him a criminal, and a year later they executed those who executed him— also for some reason. What is bad? What is good? What should one love and what hate? What does one live for? And what am I? What is life, and what is death? What power governs all?"

There was no answer to any of these questions, except one, and that not a logical answer and not at all a reply to them. The answer was: "You'll die and all will end. You'll die and know all, or cease asking." But dying was also dreadful.

The Torzhók peddler woman, in a whining voice, went on offering her wares, especially a pair of goatskin slippers. "I have hundreds of rubles I don't know what to do with, and she stands in her tattered cloak looking timidly at me," he thought. "And what does she want the money for? As if that money could add a hair's breadth to happiness or peace of mind. Can anything in the world make her or me less a prey to evil and death?—death which ends all and must come today or tomorrow—at any rate, in an instant as compared with eternity." And again he twisted the screw with the stripped thread, and again it turned uselessly in the same place.

His servant handed him a half-cut novel, in the form of letters, by Madame de Souza. He began reading about the sufferings and virtuous struggles of a certain Emilie de Mansfeld. "And why did she resist her seducer when she loved him?" he thought. "God could not have put into her heart an impulse that was against His will. My wife—as she once was—did not struggle, and perhaps she was right.

Nothing has been found out, nothing discovered," Pierre again said to himself. "All we can know is that we know nothing. And that's the height of human wisdom."

Everything within and around him seemed confused, senseless, and repellent. Yet in this very repugnance to all his circumstances Pierre found a kind of tantalizing satisfaction.

"I make bold to ask your excellency to move a little for this gentleman," said the postmaster, entering the room followed by another traveler, also detained for lack of horses.

The newcomer was a short, large-boned, yellow-faced, wrinkled old man, with gray bushy eyebrows overhanging bright eyes of an indefinite grayishcolor.

Pierre took his feet off the table, stood up, and lay down on a bed that had been got ready for him, glancing now and then at the newcomer, who, with a gloomy and tired face, was wearily taking off his wraps with the aid of his servant, and not looking at Pierre. With a pair of felt boots on his thin bony legs, and keeping on a worn, nankeen-covered, sheepskin coat, the traveler sat down on the sofa, leaned back his big head with its broad temples and close-cropped hair, and looked at Bezúkhov. The stern, shrewd, and penetrating expression of that look struck Pierre. He felt a wish to speak to the stranger, but by the time he had made up his mind to ask him a question about the roads, the traveler had closed his eyes. His shriveled old hands were folded and on the finger of one of them Pierre noticed a large cast iron ring with a seal representing a death's head. The stranger sat without stirring, either resting or, as it seemed to Pierre, sunk in profound and calm meditation. His servant was also a yellow, wrinkled old man, without beard or mustache, evidently not because he was shaven but because they had never grown. This active old servant was unpacking the traveler's canteen and preparing tea. He brought in a boiling samovar. When everything was ready, the stranger opened his eyes, moved to the table, filled a tumbler with tea for himself and one for the beardless old man to whom he passed it. Pierre began to feel a sense of uneasiness, and the need, even the inevitability, of entering into conversation with this stranger.

The servant brought back his tumbler turned upside down, * with an unfinished bit of nibbled sugar, and asked if anything more would be wanted.

* To indicate he did not want more tea.

"No. Give me the book," said the stranger.

The servant handed him a book which Pierre took to be a devotional work, and the traveler became absorbed in it. Pierre looked at him. All at once the stranger closed the book, putting in a marker, and again, leaning with his arms on the back of the sofa, sat in his former position with his eyes shut. Pierre looked at him and had not time to turn away when the old man, opening his eyes, fixed his steady and severe gaze straight on Pierre's face.

Pierre felt confused and wished to avoid that look, but the bright old eyes attracted him irresistibly.

CHAPTER II

"**I** have the pleasure of addressing Count Bezúkhov, if I am not mistaken," said the stranger in a deliberate and loud voice.

Pierre looked silently and inquiringly at him over his spectacles.

"I have heard of you, my dear sir," continued the stranger, "and of your misfortune." He seemed to emphasize the last word, as if to say—"Yes, misfortune! Call it what you please, I know that what happened to you in Moscow was a misfortune."—"I regret it very much, my dear sir."

Pierre flushed and, hurriedly putting his legs down from the bed, bent forward toward the old man with a forced and timid smile.

"I have not referred to this out of curiosity, my dear sir, but for greater reasons."

He paused, his gaze still on Pierre, and moved aside on the sofa by way of inviting the other to take a seat beside him. Pierre felt reluctant to enter into conversation with this old man, but, submitting to him involuntarily, came up and sat down beside him.

"You are unhappy, my dear sir," the stranger continued. "You are young and I am old. I should like to help you as far as lies in my power."

"Oh, yes!" said Pierre, with a forced smile. "I am very grateful to you. Where are you traveling from?"

The stranger's face was not genial, it was even cold and severe, but in spite of this, both the face and words of his new acquaintance were irresistibly attractive to Pierre.

"But if for any reason you don't feel inclined to talk to me," said the old man, "say so, my dear sir." And he suddenly smiled, in an unexpected and tenderly paternal way.

"Oh no, not at all! On the contrary, I am very glad to make your acquaintance," said Pierre. And again, glancing at the stranger's hands, he looked more closely at the ring, with its skull—a Masonic sign.

"Allow me to ask," he said, "are you a Mason?"

"Yes, I belong to the Brotherhood of the Freemasons," said the stranger, looking deeper and deeper into Pierre's eyes. "And in their name and my own I hold out a brotherly hand to you."

"I am afraid," said Pierre, smiling, and wavering between the confidence the personality of the Freemason inspired in him and his own habit of ridiculing the Masonic beliefs—"I am afraid I am very far from understanding—how am I to put it?—I am afraid my way of looking at the world is so opposed to yours that we shall not understand one another."

"I know your outlook," said the Mason, "and the view of life you mention, and which you think is the result of your own mental efforts, is the one held by the majority of people, and is the invariable fruit of pride, indolence, and ignorance. Forgive me, my dear sir, but if I had not known it I should not have addressed you. Your view of life is a regrettable delusion."

"Just as I may suppose you to be deluded," said Pierre, with a faint smile.

"I should never dare to say that I know the truth," said the Mason, whose words struck Pierre more and more by their precision and firmness. "No one can attain to truth by himself. Only by laying stone on stone with the cooperation of all, by the millions of generations from our forefather Adam to our own times, is that temple reared which is to be a worthy dwelling place of the Great God," he added, and closed his eyes.

"I ought to tell you that I do not believe... do not believe in God," said Pierre, regretfully and with an effort, feeling it essential to speak the whole truth.

The Mason looked intently at Pierre and smiled as a rich man with millions in hand might smile at a poor fellow who told him that he, poor man, had not the five rubles that would make him happy.

"Yes, you do not know Him, my dear sir," said the Mason. "You cannot know Him. You do not know Him and that is why you are unhappy."

"Yes, yes, I am unhappy," assented Pierre. "But what am I to do?"

"You know Him not, my dear sir, and so you are very unhappy. You do not know Him, but He is here, He is in me, He is in my words, He is in thee, and even in those blasphemous words thou hast just uttered!" pronounced the Mason in a stern and tremulous voice.

He paused and sighed, evidently trying to calm himself.

"If He were not," he said quietly, "you and I would not be speaking of Him, my dear sir. Of what, of whom, are we speaking? Whom hast thou denied?" he suddenly asked with exulting austerity and authority in his voice. "Who invented Him, if He did not exist? Whence came thy conception of the existence of such an incomprehensible Being? didst thou, and why did the whole world, conceive the idea of the existence of such an incomprehensible Being, a Being all-powerful, eternal, and infinite in all His attributes?..."

He stopped and remained silent for a long time.

Pierre could not and did not wish to break this silence.

"He exists, but to understand Him is hard," the Mason began again, looking not at Pierre but straight before him, and turning the leaves of his book with his old hands which from excitement he could not keep still. "If it were a man whose existence thou didst doubt I could bring him to thee, could take him by the hand and show him to thee. But how can I, an insignificant mortal, show His omnipotence, His infinity, and all His mercy to one who is blind, or who shuts his eyes that he may not see or understand Him and may not see or understand his own vileness and sinfulness?" He paused again. "Who art thou? Thou dreamest that thou art wise because thou couldst utter those blasphemous words," he went on, with a somber and scornful smile. "And thou art more foolish and unreasonable than a little child, who, playing with the parts of a skillfully made watch, dares to say that, as he does not understand its use, he does not believe in the master who made it. To know Him is hard.... For ages, from our forefather Adam to our own day, we labor to attain that knowledge and are still infinitely far from our aim; but in our lack of understanding we see only our weakness and His greatness...."

Pierre listened with swelling heart, gazing into the Mason's face with shining eyes, not interrupting or questioning him, but believing with his whole soul what the stranger said. Whether he accepted the wise reasoning contained in the Mason's words, or believed as a child believes, in the speaker's tone of conviction and earnestness, or the tremor of the speaker's voice—which sometimes almost broke—or those brilliant aged eyes grown old in this conviction, or the calm firmness and certainty of his vocation, which radiated from his whole being (and which struck Pierre especially by contrast with his own dejection and hopelessness)—at any rate, Pierre longed with his whole soul to believe and he did believe, and felt a joyful sense of comfort, regeneration, and return to life.

"He is not to be apprehended by reason, but by life," said the Mason.

"I do not understand," said Pierre, feeling with dismay doubts reawakening. He was afraid of any want of clearness, any weakness, in the Mason's arguments; he dreaded not to be able to believe in him. "I don't understand," he said, "how it is that the mind of man cannot attain the knowledge of which you speak."

The Mason smiled with his gentle fatherly smile.

"The highest wisdom and truth are like the purest liquid we may wish to imbibe," he said. "Can I receive that pure liquid into an impure vessel and judge of its purity? Only by the inner purification of myself can I retain in some degree of purity the liquid I receive."

"Yes, yes, that is so," said Pierre joyfully.

"The highest wisdom is not founded on reason alone, not on those worldly sciences of physics, history, chemistry, and the like, into which intellectual knowledge is divided. The highest wisdom is one. The highest wisdom has but one science—the science of the whole—the science explaining the whole creation and man's place in it. To receive that science it is necessary to purify and renew one's inner self, and so before one can know, it is necessary to believe and to perfect one's self. And to attain this end, we have the light called conscience that God has implanted in our souls."

"Yes, yes," assented Pierre.

"Look then at thy inner self with the eyes of the spirit, and ask thyself whether thou art content with thyself. What hast thou attained relying on reason only? What art thou? You are young, you are rich, you are clever, you are well educated. And what have you done with all these good gifts? Are you content with yourself and with your life?"

"No, I hate my life," Pierre muttered, wincing.

"Thou hatest it. Then change it, purify thyself; and as thou art purified, thou wilt gain wisdom. Look at your life, my dear sir. How have you spent it? In riotous orgies and debauchery, receiving everything from society and giving nothing in return. You have become the possessor of wealth. How have you used it? What have you done for your neighbor? Have you ever thought of your tens of thousands of slaves? Have you helped them physically and morally? No! You have profited by their toil to lead a profligate life. That is what you have done. Have you chosen a post in which you might be of service to your neighbor? No! You have spent your life in idleness. Then you married, my dear sir—took on yourself responsibility for the guidance of a young woman; and what have you done? You have not helped her to find the way of truth, my dear sir, but have thrust her into an abyss of deceit and misery. A man offended you and you shot him, and you say you do not know God and hate your life. There is nothing strange in that, my dear sir!"

After these words, the Mason, as if tired by his long discourse, again leaned his arms on the back of the sofa and closed his eyes. Pierre looked at that aged, stern, motionless, almost lifeless face and moved his lips without uttering a sound. He wished to say, "Yes, a vile, idle, vicious life!" but dared not break the silence.

The Mason cleared his throat huskily, as old men do, and called his servant.

"How about the horses?" he asked, without looking at Pierre.

"The exchange horses have just come," answered the servant. "Will you not rest here?"

"No, tell them to harness."

"Can he really be going away leaving me alone without having told me all, and without promising to help me?" thought Pierre, rising with downcast head; and he began to pace the room, glancing occasionally at the Mason. "Yes, I never thought of it, but I have led a contemptible and profligate life, though I did not like it and did not want to," thought Pierre. "But this man knows the truth and, if he wished to, could disclose it to me."

Pierre wished to say this to the Mason, but did not dare to. The traveler, having packed his things with his practiced hands, began fastening his coat. When he had finished, he turned to Bezúkhov, and said in a tone of indifferent politeness:

"Where are you going to now, my dear sir?"

"I?... I'm going to Petersburg," answered Pierre, in a childlike, hesitating voice. "I thank you. I agree with all you have said. But do not suppose me to be so bad. With my whole soul I wish to be what you would have me be, but I have never had help from anyone.... But it is I, above all, who am to blame for everything. Help me, teach me, and perhaps I may..."

Pierre could not go on. He gulped and turned away.

The Mason remained silent for a long time, evidently considering.

"Help comes from God alone," he said, "but such measure of help as our Order can bestow it will render you, my dear sir. You are going to Petersburg. Hand this to Count Willarski" (he took out his notebook and wrote a few words on a large sheet of paper folded in four). "Allow me to give you a piece of advice. When you reach the capital, first of all devote some time to solitude and self-examination and do not resume your former way of life. And now I wish you a good journey, my dear sir," he added, seeing that his servant had entered... "and success."

The traveler was Joseph AlexéevichBazdéev, as Pierre saw from the postmaster's book. Bazdéev had been one of the best-known Freemasons and Martinists, even in Novíkov's time. For a long while after he had gone, Pierre did not go to bed or order horses but paced up and down the room, pondering over his vicious past, and with a rapturous sense of beginning anew pictured to himself the blissful, irreproachable, virtuous future that seemed to him so easy. It seemed to him that he had been vicious only because he had somehow forgotten how good it is to be virtuous. Not a trace of his former doubts remained in his soul. He firmly believed in the possibility of the brotherhood of men united in the aim of supporting one another in the path of virtue, and that is how Freemasonry presented itself to him.

CHAPTER III

On reaching Petersburg Pierre did not let anyone know of his arrival, he went nowhere and spent whole days in reading Thomas à Kempis, whose book had been sent him by someone unknown. One thing he continually realized as he read that book: the joy, hitherto unknown to him, of believing in the possibility of attaining perfection, and in the possibility of active brotherly love among men, which Joseph Alexéevich had revealed to him. A week after his arrival, the young Polish count, Willarski, whom Pierre had known slightly in Petersburg society, came into his room one evening in the official and ceremonious manner in which Dólokhov's second had called on him, and, having closed the door behind him and satisfied himself that there was nobody else in the room, addressed Pierre.

"I have come to you with a message and an offer, Count," he said without sitting down. "A person of very high standing in our Brotherhood has made application for you to be received into our Order before the usual term and has proposed to me to be your sponsor. I consider it a sacred duty to fulfill that person's wishes. Do you wish to enter the Brotherhood of Freemasons under my sponsorship?"

The cold, austere tone of this man, whom he had almost always before met at balls, amiably smiling in the society of the most brilliant women, surprised Pierre.

"Yes, I do wish it," said he.

Willarski bowed his head.

"One more question, Count," he said, "which I beg you to answer in all sincerity—not as a future Mason but as an honest man: have you renounced your former convictions—do you believe in God?"

Pierre considered.

"Yes... yes, I believe in God," he said.

"In that case..." began Willarski, but Pierre interrupted him.

"Yes, I do believe in God," he repeated.

"In that case we can go," said Willarski. "My carriage is at your service."

Willarski was silent throughout the drive. To Pierre's inquiries as to what he must do and how he should answer, Willarski only replied that brothers more worthy than he would test him and that Pierre had only to tell the truth.

Having entered the courtyard of a large house where the Lodge had its headquarters, and having ascended a dark staircase, they entered a small well-lit anteroom where they took off their cloaks without the aid of a servant. From there they passed into another room. A man in strange attire appeared at the door. Willarski, stepping toward him, said something to him in French in an undertone and then went up to a small wardrobe in which Pierre noticed garments such as he had never seen before. Having taken a kerchief from the cupboard, Willarski bound Pierre's eyes with it and tied it in a knot behind, catching some hairs painfully in the knot. Then he drew his face down, kissed him, and taking him by the hand led him forward. The hairs tied in the knot hurt Pierre and there were lines of pain on his face and a shamefaced smile. His huge figure, with arms hanging down and with a puckered, though smiling face, moved after Willarski with uncertain, timid steps.

Having led him about ten paces, Willarski stopped.

"Whatever happens to you," he said, "you must bear it all manfully if you have firmly resolved to join our Brotherhood." (Pierre nodded affirmatively.) "When you hear a knock at the door, you will uncover your eyes," added Willarski. "I wish you courage and success," and, pressing Pierre's hand, he went out.

Left alone, Pierre went on smiling in the same way. Once or twice he shrugged his shoulders and raised his hand to the kerchief, as if wishing to take it off, but let it drop again. The five minutes spent with his eyes bandaged seemed to him an hour. His arms felt numb, his legs almost gave way, it seemed to him that he was tired out. He experienced a variety of most complex sensations. He felt afraid of what would happen to him and still more afraid of showing his fear. He felt curious to know what was going to happen and what would be revealed to him; but most of all, he felt joyful that the moment had come when he would at last start on that path of regeneration and on the actively virtuous life of which he had been dreaming since he met Joseph Alexéevich. Loud knocks were heard at the door. Pierre took the bandage off his eyes and glanced around him. The room was in black darkness, only a small lamp was burning inside something white. Pierre went nearer and saw that the lamp stood on a black table on which lay an open book. The book was the Gospel, and the white thing with the lamp inside was a human skull with its cavities and teeth. After reading the first words of the Gospel: "In the beginning was the Word and the Word was with God," Pierre went round the table and saw a large open box filled with something. It was a coffin with bones inside. He was not at all surprised by what he saw. Hoping to enter on an entirely new life quite unlike the old one, he expected everything to be unusual, even more unusual than what he was seeing. A skull, a coffin, the Gospel—it seemed to him that he had expected all this and even more. Trying to stimulate his emotions he looked around. "God, death, love, the brotherhood of man," he kept saying to himself, associating these words with vague yet joyful ideas. The door opened and someone came in.

By the dim light, to which Pierre had already become accustomed, he saw a rather short man. Having evidently come from the light into the darkness, the man paused, then moved with cautious steps toward the table and placed on it his small leather-gloved hands.

This short man had on a white leather apron which covered his chest and part of his legs; he had on a kind of necklace above which rose a high white ruffle, outlining his rather long face which was lit up from below.

"For what have you come hither?" asked the newcomer, turning in Pierre's direction at a slight rustle made by the latter. "Why have you, who do not believe in the truth of the light and who have not seen the light, come here? What do you seek from us? Wisdom, virtue, enlightenment?"

At the moment the door opened and the stranger came in, Pierre felt a sense of awe and veneration such as he had experienced in his boyhood at confession; he felt himself in the presence of one socially a complete stranger, yet nearer to him through the brotherhood of man. With bated breath and beating heart he moved toward the Rhetor (by which name the brother who prepared a seeker for entrance into the Brotherhood was known). Drawing nearer, he recognized in the Rhetor a man he knew, Smolyanínov, and it mortified him to think that the newcomer was an acquaintance—he wished him simply a brother and a virtuous instructor. For a long time he could not utter a word, so that the Rhetor had to repeat his question.

"Yes... I... I... desire regeneration," Pierre uttered with difficulty.

"Very well," said Smolyanínov, and went on at once: "Have you any idea of the means by which our holy Order will help you to reach your aim?" said he quietly and quickly.

"I... hope... for guidance... help... in regeneration," said Pierre, with a trembling voice and some difficulty in utterance due to his excitement and to being unaccustomed to speak of abstract matters in Russian.

"What is your conception of Freemasonry?"

"I imagine that Freemasonry is the fraternity and equality of men who have virtuous aims," said Pierre, feeling ashamed of the inadequacy of his words for the solemnity of the moment, as he spoke. "I imagine..."

"Good!" said the Rhetor quickly, apparently satisfied with this answer. "Have you sought for means of attaining your aim in religion?"

"No, I considered it erroneous and did not follow it," said Pierre, so softly that the Rhetor did not hear him and asked him what he was saying. "I have been an atheist," answered Pierre.

"You are seeking for truth in order to follow its laws in your life, therefore you seek wisdom and virtue. Is that not so?" said the Rhetor, after a moment's pause.

"Yes, yes," assented Pierre.

The Rhetor cleared his throat, crossed his gloved hands on his breast, and began to speak.

"Now I must disclose to you the chief aim of our Order," he said, "and if this aim coincides with yours, you may enter our Brotherhood with profit. The first and chief object of our Order, the foundation on which it rests and which no human power can destroy, is the preservation and handing on to posterity of a certain important mystery... which has come down to us from the remotest ages, even from the first man—a mystery on which perhaps the fate of mankind depends. But since this mystery is of such a nature that nobody can know or use it unless he be prepared by long and diligent self-purification, not everyone can hope to attain it quickly. Hence we have a secondary aim, that of preparing our members as much as possible to reform their hearts, to purify and enlighten their minds, by means handed on to us by tradition from those who have striven to attain this mystery, and thereby to render them capable of receiving it.

"By purifying and regenerating our members we try, thirdly, to improve the whole human race, offering it in our members an example of piety and virtue, and thereby try with all our might to combat the evil which sways the world. Think this over and I will come to you again."

"To combat the evil which sways the world..." Pierre repeated, and a mental image of his future activity in this direction rose in his mind. He imagined men such as he had himself been a fortnight ago, and he addressed an edifying exhortation to them. He imagined to himself vicious and unfortunate people whom he would assist by word and deed, imagined oppressors whose victims he would rescue. Of the three objects mentioned by the Rhetor, this last, that of improving mankind, especially appealed to Pierre. The important mystery mentioned by the Rhetor, though it aroused his curiosity, did not seem to him essential, and the second aim, that of purifying and regenerating himself, did not much interest him because at that moment he felt with delight that he was already perfectly cured of his former faults and was ready for all that was good.

Half an hour later, the Rhetor returned to inform the seeker of the seven virtues, corresponding to the seven steps of Solomon's temple, which every Freemason should cultivate in himself. These virtues were: 1. *Discretion*, the keeping of the secrets of the Order. 2. *Obedience* to those of higher ranks in the Order. 3. *Morality*. 4. *Love of mankind*. 5. *Courage*. 6. *Generosity*. 7. *The love of death*.

"In the seventh place, try, by the frequent thought of death," the Rhetor said, "to bring yourself to regard it not as a dreaded foe, but as a friend that frees the soul grown weary in the labors of virtue from this distressful life, and leads it to its place of recompense and peace."

"Yes, that must be so," thought Pierre, when after these words the Rhetor went away, leaving him to solitary meditation. "It must be so, but I am still so weak that I love my life, the meaning of which is only now gradually opening before me." But five of the other virtues which Pierre recalled, counting them on his fingers, he felt already in his soul: *courage, generosity, morality, love of mankind*, and especially *obedience*—which did not even seem to him a virtue, but a joy. (He now felt so glad to be free from his own lawlessness and to submit his will to those who knew the indubitable truth.) He forgot what the seventh virtue was and could not recall it.

The third time the Rhetor came back more quickly and asked Pierre whether he was still firm in his intention and determined to submit to all that would be required of him.

"I am ready for everything," said Pierre.

"I must also inform you," said the Rhetor, "that our Order delivers its teaching not in words only but also by other means, which may perhaps have a stronger effect on the sincere seeker after wisdom and virtue than mere words. This chamber with what you see therein should already have suggested to your heart, if it is sincere, more than words could do. You will perhaps also see in your further initiation a like method of enlightenment. Our Order imitates the ancient societies that explained their teaching by hieroglyphics. A hieroglyph," said the Rhetor, "is an emblem of something not cognizable by the senses but which possesses qualities resembling those of the symbol."

Pierre knew very well what a hieroglyph was, but dared not speak. He listened to the Rhetor in silence, feeling from all he said that his ordeal was about to begin.

"If you are resolved, I must begin your initiation," said the Rhetor coming closer to Pierre. "In token of generosity I ask you to give me all your valuables."

"But I have nothing here," replied Pierre, supposing that he was asked to give up all he possessed.

"What you have with you: watch, money, rings...."

War and Peace

Pierre quickly took out his purse and watch, but could not manage for some time to get the wedding ring off his fat finger. When that had been done, the Rhetor said:

"In token of obedience, I ask you to undress."

Pierre took off his coat, waistcoat, and left boot according to the Rhetor's instructions. The Mason drew the shirt back from Pierre's left breast, and stooping down pulled up the left leg of his trousers to above the knee. Pierre hurriedly began taking off his right boot also and was going to tuck up the other trouser leg to save this stranger the trouble, but the Mason told him that was not necessary and gave him a slipper for his left foot. With a childlike smile of embarrassment, doubt, and self-derision, which appeared on his face against his will, Pierre stood with his arms hanging down and legs apart, before his brother Rhetor, and awaited his further commands.

"And now, in token of candor, I ask you to reveal to me your chief passion," said the latter.

"My passion! I have had so many," replied Pierre.

"That passion which more than all others caused you to waver on the path of virtue," said the Mason.

Pierre paused, seeking a reply.

"Wine? Gluttony? Idleness? Laziness? Irritability? Anger? Women?" He went over his vices in his mind, not knowing to which of them to give the pre-eminence.

"Women," he said in a low, scarcely audible voice.

The Mason did not move and for a long time said nothing after this answer. At last he moved up to Pierre and, taking the kerchief that lay on the table, again bound his eyes.

"For the last time I say to you—turn all your attention upon yourself, put a bridle on your senses, and seek blessedness, not in passion but in your own heart. The source of blessedness is not without us but within...."

Pierre had already long been feeling in himself that refreshing source of blessedness which now flooded his heart with glad emotion.

CHAPTER IV

Soon after this there came into the dark chamber to fetch Pierre, not the Rhetor but Pierre's sponsor, Willarski, whom he recognized by his voice. To fresh questions as to the firmness of his resolution Pierre replied: "Yes, yes, I agree," and with a beaming, childlike smile, his fat chest uncovered, stepping unevenly and timidly in one slippered and one booted foot, he advanced, while Willarski held a sword to his bare chest. He was conducted from that room along passages that turned backwards and forwards and was at last brought to the doors of the Lodge. Willarski coughed, he was answered by the Masonic knock with mallets, the doors opened before them. A bass voice (Pierre was still blindfolded) questioned him as to who he was, when and where he was born, and so on. Then he was again led somewhere still blindfolded, and as they went along he was told allegories of the toils of his pilgrimage, of holy friendship, of the Eternal Architect of the universe, and of the courage with which he should endure toils and dangers. During these wanderings, Pierre noticed that he was spoken of now as the "Seeker," now as the "Sufferer," and now as the "Postulant," to the accompaniment of various knockings with mallets and swords. As he was being led up to some object he noticed a hesitation and uncertainty among his conductors. He heard those around him disputing in whispers and one of them insisting that he should be led along a certain carpet. After that they took his right hand, placed it on something, and told him to hold a pair of compasses to his left breast with the other hand and to repeat after someone who read aloud an oath of fidelity to the laws of the Order. The candles were then extinguished and some spirit lighted, as Pierre knew by the smell, and he was told that he would now see the lesser light. The bandage was taken off his eyes and, by the faint light of the burning spirit, Pierre, as in a dream, saw several men standing before him, wearing aprons like the Rhetor's and holding swords in their hands pointed at his breast. Among them stood a man whose white shirt was stained with blood. On seeing this, Pierre moved forward with his breast toward the swords, meaning them to pierce it. But the swords were drawn back from him and he was at once blindfolded again.

"Now thou hast seen the lesser light," uttered a voice. Then the candles were relit and he was told that he would see the full light; the bandage was again removed and more than ten voices said together: *"Sic transit gloria mundi."*

Pierre gradually began to recover himself and looked about at the room and at the people in it. Round a long table covered with black sat some twelve men in garments like those he had already seen. Some of them Pierre had met in Petersburg society. In the President's chair sat a young man he did not know, with a peculiar cross hanging from his neck. On his right sat the Italian abbé whom Pierre had met at Anna Pávlovna's two years before. There were also present a very distinguished dignitary and a Swiss who had formerly been tutor at the Kurágins'. All maintained a solemn silence, listening to the words of the President, who held a mallet in his hand. Let into the wall was a star-shaped light. At one side of the table was a small carpet with various figures worked upon it, at the other was something resembling an altar on which lay a Testament and a skull. Round it stood seven large candlesticks like those used in churches. Two of the brothers led Pierre up to the altar, placed his feet at right angles, and bade him lie down, saying that he must prostrate himself at the Gates of the Temple.

"He must first receive the trowel," whispered one of the brothers.

"Oh, hush, please!" said another.

Pierre, perplexed, looked round with his shortsighted eyes without obeying, and suddenly doubts arose in his mind. "Where am I? What am I doing? Aren't they laughing at me? Shan't I be ashamed to remember this?" But these doubts only lasted a moment. Pierre glanced at the serious faces of those around, remembered all he had already gone through, and realized that he could not stop halfway. He was aghast at his hesitation and, trying to arouse his former devotional feeling, prostrated himself before the Gates of the Temple.

And really, the feeling of devotion returned to him even more strongly than before. When he had lain there some time, he was told to get up, and a white leather apron, such as the others wore, was put on him: he was given a trowel and three pairs of gloves, and then the Grand Master addressed him. He told him that he should try to do nothing to stain the whiteness of that apron, which symbolized strength and purity; then of the unexplained trowel, he told him to toil with it to cleanse his own heart from vice, and indulgently to smooth with it the heart of his neighbor. As to the first pair of gloves, a man's, he said that Pierre could not know their meaning but must keep them. The second pair of man's gloves he was to wear at the meetings, and finally of the third, a pair of women's gloves, he said: "Dear brother, these woman's gloves are intended for you too. Give them to the woman whom you shall honor most of all. This gift will be a pledge of your purity of heart to her whom you select to be your worthy helpmeet in Masonry." And after a pause, he added: "But beware, dear brother, that these gloves do not deck hands that are unclean." While the Grand Master said these last words it seemed to Pierre that he grew embarrassed. Pierre himself grew still more confused, blushed like a child till tears came to his eyes, began looking about him uneasily, and an awkward pause followed.

This silence was broken by one of the brethren, who led Pierre up to the rug and began reading to him from a manuscript book an explanation of all the figures on it: the sun, the moon, a hammer, a plumb line, a trowel, a rough stone and a squared stone, a pillar, three windows, and so on. Then a place was assigned to Pierre, he was shown the signs of the Lodge, told the password, and at last was permitted to sit down. The Grand Master began reading the statutes. They were very long, and Pierre, from joy, agitation, and embarrassment, was not in a state to understand what was being read. He managed to follow only the last words of the statutes and these remained in his mind.

"In our temples we recognize no other distinctions," read the Grand Master, "but those between virtue and vice. Beware of making any distinctions which may infringe equality. Fly to a brother's aid whoever he may be, exhort him who goeth astray, raise him that falleth, never bear malice or enmity toward thy brother. Be kindly and courteous. Kindle in all hearts the flame of virtue. Share thy happiness with thy neighbor, and may envy never dim the purity of that bliss. Forgive thy enemy, do not avenge thyself except by doing him good. Thus fulfilling the highest law thou shalt regain traces of the ancient dignity which thou hast lost."

He finished and, getting up, embraced and kissed Pierre, who, with tears of joy in his eyes, looked round him, not knowing how to answer the congratulations and greetings from acquaintances that met him on all sides. He acknowledged no acquaintances but saw in all these men only brothers, and burned with impatience to set to work with them.

The Grand Master rapped with his mallet. All the Masons sat down in their places, and one of them read an exhortation on the necessity of humility.

The Grand Master proposed that the last duty should be performed, and the distinguished dignitary who bore the title of "Collector of Alms" went round to all the brothers. Pierre would have liked to subscribe all he had, but fearing that it might look like pride subscribed the same amount as the others.

The meeting was at an end, and on reaching home Pierre felt as if he had returned from a long journey on which he had spent dozens of years, had become completely changed, and had quite left behind his former habits and way of life.

CHAPTER V

The day after he had been received into the Lodge, Pierre was sitting at home reading a book and trying to fathom the significance of the Square, one side of which symbolized God, another moral things, a third physical things, and the fourth a combination of these. Now and then his attention wandered from the book and the Square and he formed in imagination a new plan of life. On the previous evening at the Lodge, he had heard that a rumor of his duel had reached the Emperor and that it would be wiser for him to leave Petersburg. Pierre proposed going to his estates in the south and there attending to the welfare of his serfs. He was joyfully planning this new life, when Prince Vasíli suddenly entered the room.

"My dear fellow, what have you been up to in Moscow? Why have you quarreled with Hélène, *moncher?* You are under a delusion," said Prince Vasíli, as he entered. "I know all about it, and I can tell you positively that Hélène is as innocent before you as Christ was before the Jews."

Pierre was about to reply, but Prince Vasíli interrupted him.

"And why didn't you simply come straight to me as to a friend? I know all about it and understand it all," he said. "You behaved as becomes a man who values his honor, perhaps too hastily, but we won't go into that. But consider the position in which you are placing her and me in the eyes of society, and even of the court," he added, lowering his voice. "She is living in Moscow and you are here. Remember, dear boy," and he drew Pierre's arm downwards, "it is simply a misunderstanding. I expect you feel it so yourself. Let us write her a letter at once, and she'll come here and all will be explained, or else, my dear boy, let me tell you it's quite likely you'll have to suffer for it."

Prince Vasíli gave Pierre a significant look.

"I know from reliable sources that the Dowager Empress is taking a keen interest in the whole affair. You know she is very gracious to Hélène."

Pierre tried several times to speak, but, on one hand, Prince Vasíli did not let him and, on the other, Pierre himself feared to begin to speak in the tone of decided refusal and disagreement in which he had firmly resolved to answer his father-in-law. Moreover, the words of the Masonic statutes, "be kindly and courteous," recurred to him. He blinked, went red, got up and sat down again, struggling with himself to do what was for him the most difficult thing in life—to say an unpleasant thing to a man's face, to say what the other, whoever he might be, did not expect. He was so used to submitting to Prince Vasíli's tone of careless self-assurance that he felt he would be unable to withstand it now, but he also felt that on what he said now his future depended—whether he would follow the same old road, or that new path so attractively shown him by the Masons, on which he firmly believed he would be reborn to a new life.

"Now, dear boy," said Prince Vasíli playfully, "say 'yes,' and I'll write to her myself, and we will kill the fatted calf."

But before Prince Vasíli had finished his playful speech, Pierre, without looking at him, and with a kind of fury that made him like his father, muttered in a whisper:

"Prince, I did not ask you here. Go, please go!" And he jumped up and opened the door for him.

"Go!" he repeated, amazed at himself and glad to see the look of confusion and fear that showed itself on Prince Vasíli's face.

"What's the matter with you? Are you ill?"

"Go!" the quivering voice repeated. And Prince Vasíli had to go without receiving any explanation.

A week later, Pierre, having taken leave of his new friends, the Masons, and leaving large sums of money with them for alms, went away to his estates. His new brethren gave him letters to the Kiev and Odessa Masons and promised to write to him and guide him in his new activity.

CHAPTER VI

The duel between Pierre and Dólokhov was hushed up and, in spite of the Emperor's severity regarding duels at that time, neither the principals nor their seconds suffered for it. But the story of the duel, confirmed by Pierre's rupture with his wife, was the talk of society. Pierre who had been regarded with patronizing condescension when he was an illegitimate son, and petted and extolled when he was the best match in Russia, had sunk greatly in the esteem of society after his marriage—when the marriageable daughters and their mothers had nothing to hope from him—especially as he did not know how, and did not wish, to court society's favor. Now he alone was blamed for what had happened, he was said to be insanely jealous and subject like his father to fits of bloodthirsty rage. And when after Pierre's departure Hélène returned to Petersburg, she was received by all her acquaintances not only cordially, but even with a shade of deference due to her misfortune. When conversation turned on her husband Hélène assumed a dignified expression, which with characteristic tact she had acquired though she did not understand its significance. This expression suggested that she had resolved to endure her troubles uncomplainingly and that her husband was a cross laid upon her by God. Prince Vasíli expressed his opinion more openly. He shrugged his shoulders when Pierre was mentioned and, pointing to his forehead, remarked:

"A bit touched—I always said so."

"I said from the first," declared Anna Pávlovna referring to Pierre, "I said at the time and before anyone else" (she insisted on her priority) "that that senseless young man was spoiled by the depraved ideas of these days. I said so even at the time when everybody was in raptures about him, when he had just returned from abroad, and when, if you remember, he posed as a sort of Marat at one of my soirees. And how has it ended? I was against this marriage even then and foretold all that has happened."

Anna Pávlovna continued to give on free evenings the same kind of soirees as before—such as she alone had the gift of arranging—at which was to be found "the cream of really good society, the bloom of the intellectual essence of Petersburg," as she herself put it. Besides this refined selection of society Anna Pávlovna's receptions were also distinguished by the fact that she always presented some new and interesting person to the visitors and that nowhere else was the state of the political thermometer of legitimate Petersburg court society so dearly and distinctly indicated.

Toward the end of 1806, when all the sad details of Napoleon's destruction of the Prussian army at Jena and Auerstädt and the surrender of most of the Prussian fortresses had been received, when our troops had already entered Prussia and our second war with Napoleon was beginning, Anna Pávlovna gave one of her soirees. The "cream of really good society" consisted of the fascinating Hélène, forsaken by her husband, Mortemart, the delightful Prince Hippolyte who had just returned from Vienna, two diplomatists, the old aunt, a young man referred to in that drawing room as "a man of great merit" (*un homme de beaucoup de mérite*), a newly appointed maid of honor and her mother, and several other less noteworthy persons.

The novelty Anna Pávlovna was setting before her guests that evening was BorísDrubetskóy, who had just arrived as a special messenger from the Prussian army and was aide-de-camp to a very important personage.

The temperature shown by the political thermometer to the company that evening was this:

"Whatever the European sovereigns and commanders may do to countenance Bonaparte, and to cause *me*, and *us* in general, annoyance and mortification, our opinion of Bonaparte cannot alter. We shall not cease to express our sincere views on that subject, and can only say to the King of Prussia and others: 'So much the worse for you. *Tu l'as voulu, George Dandin,*' that's all we have to say about it!"

When Borís, who was to be served up to the guests, entered the drawing room, almost all the company had assembled, and the conversation, guided by Anna Pávlovna, was about our diplomatic relations with Austria and the hope of an alliance with her.

Borís, grown more manly and looking fresh, rosy and self-possessed, entered the drawing room elegantly dressed in the uniform of an aide-de-camp and was duly conducted to pay his respects to the aunt and then brought back to the general circle.

Anna Pávlovna gave him her shriveled hand to kiss and introduced him to several persons whom he did not know, giving him a whispered description of each.

"Prince Hippolyte Kurágin—charming young fellow; M. Kronq,—chargé d'affaires from Copenhagen—a profound intellect," and simply, "Mr. Shítov—a man of great merit"—this of the man usually so described.

Thanks to Anna Mikháylovna's efforts, his own tastes, and the peculiarities of his reserved nature, Borís had managed during his service to place himself very advantageously. He was aide-de-camp to a very important personage, had been sent on a very important mission to Prussia, and had just returned from there as a special messenger. He had become thoroughly conversant with that unwritten code with which he had been so pleased at Olmütz and according to which an ensign might rank incomparably higher than a general, and according to which what was needed for success in the service was not effort or work, or courage, or perseverance, but only the knowledge of how to get on with those who can grant rewards, and he was himself often surprised at the rapidity of his success and at the inability of others to understand these things. In consequence of this discovery his whole manner of life, all his relations with old friends, all his plans for his future, were completely altered. He was not rich, but would spend his last groat to be better dressed than others, and would rather deprive himself of many pleasures than allow himself to be seen in a shabby equipage or appear in the streets of Petersburg in an old uniform. He made friends with and sought the acquaintance of only those above him in position and who could therefore be of use to him. He liked Petersburg and despised Moscow. The remembrance of the Rostóvs' house and of his childish love for Natásha was unpleasant to him and he had not once been to see the Rostóvs since the day of his departure for the army. To be in Anna

Pávlovna's drawing room he considered an important step up in the service, and he at once understood his role, letting his hostess make use of whatever interest he had to offer. He himself carefully scanned each face, appraising the possibilities of establishing intimacy with each of those present, and the advantages that might accrue. He took the seat indicated to him beside the fair Hélène and listened to the general conversation.

"Vienna considers the bases of the proposed treaty so unattainable that not even a continuity of most brilliant successes would secure them, and she doubts the means we have of gaining them. That is the actual phrase used by the Vienna cabinet," said the Danish chargé d'affaires.

"The doubt is flattering," said "the man of profound intellect," with a subtle smile.

"We must distinguish between the Vienna cabinet and the Emperor of Austria," said Mortemart. "The Emperor of Austria can never have thought of such a thing, it is only the cabinet that says it."

"Ah, my dear vicomte," put in Anna Pávlovna, *"L'Urope"* (for some reason she called it *Urope* as if that were a specially refined French pronunciation which she could allow herself when conversing with a Frenchman), *"L'Urope ne sera jamais notrealliéesincère."* *

* "Europe will never be our sincere ally."

After that Anna Pávlovna led up to the courage and firmness of the King of Prussia, in order to draw Borís into the conversation.

Borís listened attentively to each of the speakers, awaiting his turn, but managed meanwhile to look round repeatedly at his neighbor, the beautiful Hélène, whose eyes several times met those of the handsome young aide-de-camp with a smile.

Speaking of the position of Prussia, Anna Pávlovna very naturally asked Borís to tell them about his journey to Glogau and in what state he found the Prussian army. Borís, speaking with deliberation, told them in pure, correct French many interesting details about the armies and the court, carefully abstaining from expressing an opinion of his own about the facts he was recounting. For some time he engrossed the general attention, and Anna Pávlovna felt that the novelty she had served up was received with pleasure by all her visitors. The greatest attention of all to Borís' narrative was shown by Hélène. She asked him several questions about his journey and seemed greatly interested in the state of the Prussian army. As soon as he had finished she turned to him with her usual smile.

"You absolutely must come and see me," she said in a tone that implied that, for certain considerations he could not know of, this was absolutely necessary.

"On Tuesday between eight and nine. It will give me great pleasure."

Borís promised to fulfill her wish and was about to begin a conversation with her, when Anna Pávlovna called him away on the pretext that her aunt wished to hear him.

"You know her husband, of course?" said Anna Pávlovna, closing her eyes and indicating Hélène with a sorrowful gesture. "Ah, she is such an unfortunate and charming woman! Don't mention him before her—please don't! It is too painful for her!"

CHAPTER VII

When Borís and Anna Pávlovna returned to the others Prince Hippolyte had the ear of the company.

Bending forward in his armchair he said: *"Le Roi de Prusse!"* and having said this laughed. Everyone turned toward him.

"Le Roi de Prusse?" Hippolyte said interrogatively, again laughing, and then calmly and seriously sat back in his chair. Anna Pávlovna waited for him to go on, but as he seemed quite decided to say no more she began to tell of how at Potsdam the impious Bonaparte had stolen the sword of Frederick the Great.

"It is the sword of Frederick the Great which I..." she began, but Hippolyte interrupted her with the words: *"Le Roi de Prusse..."* and again, as soon as all turned toward him, excused himself and said no more.

Anna Pávlovna frowned. Mortemart, Hippolyte's friend, addressed him firmly.

"Come now, what about your *Roi de Prusse?*"

Hippolyte laughed as if ashamed of laughing.

"Oh, it's nothing. I only wished to say..." (he wanted to repeat a joke he had heard in Vienna and which he had been trying all that evening to get in) "I only wished to say that we are wrong to fight *pour le Roi de Prusse!"*

Borís smiled circumspectly, so that it might be taken as ironical or appreciative according to the way the joke was received. Everybody laughed.

"Your joke is too bad, it's witty but unjust," said Anna Pávlovna, shaking her little shriveled finger at him.

"We are not fighting *pour le Roi de Prusse*, but for right principles. Oh, that wicked Prince Hippolyte!" she said.

The conversation did not flag all evening and turned chiefly on the political news. It became particularly animated toward the end of the evening when the rewards bestowed by the Emperor were mentioned.

"You know N— N— received a snuffbox with the portrait last year?" said "the man of profound intellect." "Why shouldn't S— S— get the same distinction?"

"Pardon me! A snuffbox with the Emperor's portrait is a reward but not a distinction," said the diplomatist—"a gift, rather."

"There are precedents, I may mention Schwarzenberg."

"It's impossible," replied another.

"Will you bet? The ribbon of the order is a different matter...."

When everybody rose to go, Hélène who had spoken very little all the evening again turned to Borís, asking him in a tone of caressing significant command to come to her on Tuesday.

"It is of great importance to me," she said, turning with a smile toward Anna Pávlovna, and Anna Pávlovna, with the same sad smile with which she spoke of her exalted patroness, supported Hélène's wish.

It seemed as if from some words Borís had spoken that evening about the Prussian army, Hélène had suddenly found it necessary to see him. She seemed to promise to explain that necessity to him when he came on Tuesday.

But on Tuesday evening, having come to Hélène's splendid salon, Borís received no clear explanation of why it had been necessary for him to come. There were other guests and the countess talked little to him, and only as he kissed her hand on taking leave said unexpectedly and in a whisper, with a strangely unsmiling face: "Come to dinner tomorrow... in the evening. You must come.... Come!"

During that stay in Petersburg, Borís became an intimate in the countess' house.

CHAPTER VIII

The war was flaming up and nearing the Russian frontier. Everywhere one heard curses on Bonaparte, "the enemy of mankind." Militiamen and recruits were being enrolled in the villages, and from the seat of war came contradictory news, false as usual and therefore variously interpreted. The life of old Prince Bolkónski, Prince Andrew, and Princess Mary had greatly changed since 1805.

In 1806 the old prince was made one of the eight commanders in chief then appointed to supervise the enrollment decreed throughout Russia. Despite the weakness of age, which had become particularly noticeable since the time when he thought his son had been killed, he did not think it right to refuse a duty to which he had been appointed by the Emperor himself, and this fresh opportunity for action gave him new energy and strength. He was continually traveling through the three provinces entrusted to him, was pedantic in the fulfillment of his duties, severe to cruel with his subordinates, and went into everything down to the minutest details himself. Princess Mary had ceased taking lessons in mathematics from her father, and when the old prince was at home went to his study with the wet nurse and little Prince Nicholas (as his grandfather called him). The baby Prince Nicholas lived with his wet nurse and nurse Sávishna in the late princess' rooms and Princess Mary spent most of the day in the nursery, taking a mother's place to her little nephew as best she could. Mademoiselle Bourienne, too, seemed passionately fond of the boy, and Princess Mary often deprived herself to give her friend the pleasure of dandling the little *angel*—as she called her nephew—and playing with him.

Near the altar of the church at Bald Hills there was a chapel over the tomb of the little princess, and in this chapel was a marble monument brought from Italy, representing an angel with outspread wings ready to fly upwards. The angel's upper lip was slightly raised as though about to smile, and once on coming out of the chapel Prince Andrew and Princess Mary admitted to one another that the angel's face reminded them strangely of the little princess. But what was still stranger, though of this Prince Andrew said nothing to his sister, was that in the expression the sculptor had happened to give the angel's face, Prince Andrew read the same mild reproach he had read on the face of his dead wife: "Ah, why have you done this to me?"

Soon after Prince Andrew's return the old prince made over to him a large estate, Bogucharovo, about twenty-five miles from Bald Hills. Partly because of the depressing memories associated with Bald Hills, partly because Prince Andrew did not always feel equal to bearing with his father's peculiarities, and partly because he needed solitude, Prince Andrew made use of Bogucharovo, began building and spent most of his time there.

After the Austerlitz campaign Prince Andrew had firmly resolved not to continue his military service, and when the war recommenced and everybody had to serve, he took a post under his father in the recruitment so as to avoid active service. The old prince and his son seemed to have changed roles since the campaign of 1805. The old man, roused by activity, expected the best results from the new campaign, while Prince Andrew on the contrary, taking no part in the war and secretly regretting this, saw only the dark side.

On February 26, 1807, the old prince set off on one of his circuits. Prince Andrew remained at Bald Hills as usual during his father's absence. Little Nicholas had been unwell for four days. The coachman who had driven the old prince to town returned bringing papers and letters for Prince Andrew.

Not finding the young prince in his study the valet went with the letters to Princess Mary's apartments, but did not find him there. He was told that the prince had gone to the nursery.

"If you please, your excellency, Pétrusha has brought some papers," said one of the nursemaids to Prince Andrew who was sitting on a child's little chair while, frowning and with trembling hands, he poured drops from a medicine bottle into a wineglass half full of water.

"What is it?" he said crossly, and, his hand shaking unintentionally, he poured too many drops into the glass. He threw the mixture onto the floor and asked for some more water. The maid brought it.

There were in the room a child's cot, two boxes, two armchairs, a table, a child's table, and the little chair on which Prince Andrew was sitting. The curtains were drawn, and a single candle was burning on the table, screened by a bound music book so that the light did not fall on the cot.

"My dear," said Princess Mary, addressing her brother from beside the cot where she was standing, "better wait a bit... later..."

"Oh, leave off, you always talk nonsense and keep putting things off—and this is what comes of it!" said Prince Andrew in an exasperated whisper, evidently meaning to wound his sister.

"My dear, really... it's better not to wake him... he's asleep," said the princess in a tone of entreaty.

Prince Andrew got up and went on tiptoe up to the little bed, wineglass in hand.

"Perhaps we'd really better not wake him," he said hesitating.

"As you please... really... I think so... but as you please," said Princess Mary, evidently intimidated and confused that her opinion had prevailed. She drew her brother's attention to the maid who was calling him in a whisper.

It was the second night that neither of them had slept, watching the boy who was in a high fever. These last days, mistrusting their household doctor and expecting another for whom they had sent to town, they had been trying first one remedy and then another. Worn out by sleeplessness and anxiety they threw their burden of sorrow on one another and reproached and disputed with each other.

"Pétrusha has come with papers from your father," whispered the maid.

Prince Andrew went out.

"Devil take them!" he muttered, and after listening to the verbal instructions his father had sent and taking the correspondence and his father's letter, he returned to the nursery.

"Well?" he asked.

"Still the same. Wait, for heaven's sake. Karl Ivánich always says that sleep is more important than anything," whispered Princess Mary with a sigh.

Prince Andrew went up to the child and felt him. He was burning hot.

"Confound you and your Karl Ivánich!" He took the glass with the drops and again went up to the cot.

"Andrew, don't!" said Princess Mary.

But he scowled at her angrily though also with suffering in his eyes, and stooped glass in hand over the infant.

"But I wish it," he said. "I beg you—give it him!"

Princess Mary shrugged her shoulders but took the glass submissively and calling the nurse began giving the medicine. The child screamed hoarsely. Prince Andrew winced and, clutching his head, went out and sat down on a sofa in the next room.

He still had all the letters in his hand. Opening them mechanically he began reading. The old prince, now and then using abbreviations, wrote in his large elongated hand on blue paper as follows:

Have just this moment received by special messenger very joyful news—if it's not false. Bennigsen seems to have obtained a complete victory over Buonaparte at Eylau. In Petersburg everyone is rejoicing, and the rewards sent to the army are innumerable. Though he is a German—I congratulate him! I can't make out what the commander at Kórchevo—a certain Khandrikóv—is up to; till now the additional men and provisions have not arrived. Gallop off to him at once and say I'll have his head off if everything is not here in a week. Have received another letter about the Preussisch-Eylau battle from Pétenka—he took part in it—and it's all true. When mischief-makers don't meddle even a German beats Buonaparte. He is said to be fleeing in great disorder. Mind you gallop off to Kórchevo without delay and carry out instructions!

Prince Andrew sighed and broke the seal of another envelope. It was a closely written letter of two sheets from Bilíbin. He folded it up without reading it and reread his father's letter, ending with the words: "Gallop off to Kórchevo and carry out instructions!"

"No, pardon me, I won't go now till the child is better," thought he, going to the door and looking into the nursery.

Princess Mary was still standing by the cot, gently rocking the baby.

"Ah yes, and what else did he say that's unpleasant?" thought Prince Andrew, recalling his father's letter. "Yes, we have gained a victory over Bonaparte, just when I'm not serving. Yes, yes, he's always poking fun at me.... Ah, well! Let him!" And he began reading Bilíbin's letter which was written in French. He read without understanding half of it, read only to forget, if but for a moment, what he had too long been thinking of so painfully to the exclusion of all else.

CHAPTER IX

B ilíbin was now at army headquarters in a diplomatic capacity, and though he wrote in French and used French jests and French idioms, he described the whole campaign with a fearless self-censure and self-derision genuinely Russian. Bilíbin wrote that the obligation of diplomatic discretion tormented him, and he was happy to have in Prince Andrew a reliable correspondent to whom he could pour out the bile he had accumulated at the sight of all that was being done in the army. The letter was old, having been written before the battle at Preussisch-Eylau.

"Since the day of our brilliant success at Austerlitz," wrote Bilíbin, "as you know, my dear prince, I never leave headquarters. I have certainly acquired a taste for war, and it is just as well for me; what I have seen during these last three months is incredible.

"I begin *ab ovo*. 'The enemy of the human race,' as you know, attacks the Prussians. The Prussians are our faithful allies who have only betrayed us three times in three years. We take up their cause, but it turns out that 'the enemy of the human race' pays no heed to our fine speeches and in his rude and savage way throws himself on the Prussians without giving them time to finish the parade they had begun, and in two twists of the hand he breaks them to smithereens and installs himself in the palace at Potsdam.

"'I most ardently desire,' writes the King of Prussia to Bonaparte, 'that Your Majesty should be received and treated in my palace in a manner agreeable to yourself, and in so far as circumstances allowed, I have hastened to take all steps to that end. May I have succeeded!'

The Prussian generals pride themselves on being polite to the French and lay down their arms at the first demand.

"The head of the garrison at Glogau, with ten thousand men, asks the King of Prussia what he is to do if he is summoned to surrender.... All this is absolutely true.

"In short, hoping to settle matters by taking up a warlike attitude, it turns out that we have landed ourselves in war, and what is more, in war on our own frontiers, *with* and *for* the King of Prussia. We have everything in perfect order, only one little thing is lacking, namely, a commander in chief. As it was considered that the Austerlitz success might have been more decisive had the commander in chief not been so young, all our octogenarians were reviewed, and of Prozoróvski and Kámenski the latter was preferred. The general comes to us, Suvórov-like, in a *kibítka*, and is received with acclamations of joy and triumph.

"On the 4th, the first courier arrives from Petersburg. The mails are taken to the field marshal's room, for he likes to do everything himself. I am called in to help sort the letters and take those meant for us. The field marshal looks on and waits for letters addressed to him. We search, but none are to be found. The field marshal grows impatient and sets to work himself and finds letters from the Emperor to Count T., Prince V., and others. Then he bursts into one of his wild furies and rages at everyone and everything, seizes the letters, opens them, and reads those from the Emperor addressed to others. 'Ah! So that's the way they treat me! No confidence in me! Ah, ordered to keep an eye on me! Very well then! Get along with you!' So he writes the famous order of the day to General Bennigsen:

"'I am wounded and cannot ride and consequently cannot command the army. You have brought your army corps to Pultúsk, routed: here it is exposed, and without fuel or forage, so something must be done, and, as you yourself reported to Count Buxhöwden yesterday, you must think of retreating to our frontier—which do today.'

"'From all my riding,' he writes to the Emperor, 'I have got a saddle sore which, coming after all my previous journeys, quite prevents my riding and commanding so vast an army, so I have passed on the command to the general next in seniority, Count Buxhöwden, having sent him my whole staff and all that belongs to it, advising him if there is a lack of bread, to move farther into the interior of Prussia, for only one day's ration of bread remains, and in some regiments none at all, as reported by the division commanders, Ostermann and Sedmorétzki, and all that the peasants had has been eaten up. I myself will remain in hospital at Ostrolenka till I recover. In regard to which I humbly submit my report, with the information that if the army remains in its present bivouac another fortnight there will not be a healthy man left in it by spring.

"'Grant leave to retire to his country seat to an old man who is already in any case dishonored by being unable to fulfill the great and glorious task for which he was chosen. I shall await your most gracious permission here in hospital, that I may not have to play the part of a *secretary* rather than *commander* in the army. My removal from the army does not produce the slightest stir—a blind man has left it. There are thousands such as I in Russia.'

"The field marshal is angry with the Emperor and he punishes us all, isn't it logical?

"This is the first act. Those that follow are naturally increasingly interesting and entertaining. After the field marshal's departure it appears that we are within sight of the enemy and must give battle. Buxhöwden is commander in chief by seniority, but General Bennigsen does not quite see it; more particularly as it is he and his corps who are within sight of the enemy and he wishes to profit by the opportunity to fight a battle 'on his own hand' as the Germans say. He does so. This is the battle of Pultúsk, which is considered a great victory but in my opinion was nothing of the kind. We civilians, as you know, have a very bad way of deciding whether a battle was won or lost. Those who retreat after a battle have lost it is what we say; and according to that it is we who lost the battle of Pultúsk. In short, we retreat after the battle but send a courier to Petersburg with news of a victory, and General Bennigsen, hoping to receive from Petersburg the post of commander in chief as a reward for his victory, does not give up the command of the army to General Buxhöwden. During this interregnum we begin a very original and interesting series of maneuvers. Our aim is no longer, as it should be, to avoid or attack the enemy, but solely to avoid General Buxhöwden who by right of seniority should be our chief. So energetically do we pursue this aim that after crossing an unfordable river we burn the bridges to separate ourselves from our enemy, who at the moment is not Bonaparte but Buxhöwden. General Buxhöwden was all but attacked and captured by a superior enemy force as a result of one of these maneuvers that enabled us to escape him. Buxhöwden pursues us—we scuttle. He hardly crosses the river to our side before we recross to the other. At last our enemy, Buxhöwden, catches us and attacks. Both generals are angry, and the result is a challenge on Buxhöwden's part and an epileptic fit on Bennigsen's. But at the critical moment the courier who carried the news of our victory at Pultúsk to Petersburg returns bringing our appointment as commander in chief, and our first foe, Buxhöwden, is vanquished; we can now turn our thoughts to the second, Bonaparte. But as it turns out, just at that moment a third enemy rises before us—namely the *Orthodox Russian soldiers*, loudly demanding bread, meat, biscuits, fodder, and whatnot! The stores are empty, the roads impassable. The Orthodox begin looting, and in a way of which our last campaign can give you no idea. Half the regiments form bands and scour the countryside and put everything to fire and sword. The inhabitants are totally ruined, the hospitals overflow with sick, and famine is everywhere. Twice the marauders even attack our headquarters, and the commander in chief has to ask for a battalion to disperse them. During one of these attacks they carried off my empty portmanteau and my dressing gown. The Emperor proposes to give all commanders of divisions the right to shoot marauders, but I much fear this will oblige one half the army to shoot the other."

At first Prince Andrew read with his eyes only, but after a while, in spite of himself (although he knew how far it was safe to trust Bilíbin), what he had read began to interest him more and more. When he had read thus far, he crumpled the letter up and threw it away. It was not what he had read that vexed him, but the fact that the life out there in which he had now no part could perturb him. He shut his eyes, rubbed his forehead as if to rid himself of all interest in what he had read, and listened to what was passing in the nursery. Suddenly he thought he heard a strange noise through the door. He was seized with alarm lest something should have happened to the child while he was reading the letter. He went on tiptoe to the nursery door and opened it.

Just as he went in he saw that the nurse was hiding something from him with a scared look and that Princess Mary was no longer by the cot.

"My dear," he heard what seemed to him her despairing whisper behind him.

As often happens after long sleeplessness and long anxiety, he was seized by an unreasoning panic—it occurred to him that the child was dead. All that he saw and heard seemed to confirm this terror.

"All is over," he thought, and a cold sweat broke out on his forehead. He went to the cot in confusion, sure that he would find it empty and that the nurse had been hiding the dead baby. He drew the curtain aside and for some time his frightened, restless eyes could not find the baby. At last he saw him: the rosy boy had tossed about till he lay across the bed with his head lower than the pillow, and was smacking his lips in his sleep and breathing evenly.

Prince Andrew was as glad to find the boy like that, as if he had already lost him. He bent over him and, as his sister had taught him, tried with his lips whether the child was still feverish. The soft forehead was moist. Prince Andrew touched the head with his hand; even the hair was wet, so profusely had the child perspired. He was not dead, but evidently the crisis was over and he was convalescent. Prince Andrew longed to snatch up, to squeeze, to hold to his heart, this helpless little creature, but dared not do so. He stood over him, gazing at his head and at the little arms and legs which showed under the blanket. He heard a rustle behind him and a shadow appeared under the curtain of the cot. He did not look round, but still gazing at the infant's face listened to his regular breathing. The dark shadow was Princess Mary, who had come up to the cot with noiseless steps, lifted the curtain, and dropped it again behind her. Prince Andrew recognized her without looking and held out his hand to her. She pressed it.

"He has perspired," said Prince Andrew.

"I was coming to tell you so."

The child moved slightly in his sleep, smiled, and rubbed his forehead against the pillow.

Prince Andrew looked at his sister. In the dim shadow of the curtain her luminous eyes shone more brightly than usual from the tears of joy that were in them. She leaned over to her brother and kissed him, slightly catching the curtain of the cot. Each made the other a warning gesture and stood still in the dim light beneath the curtain as if not wishing to leave that seclusion where they three were shut off from all the world. Prince Andrew was the first to move away, ruffling his hair against the muslin of the curtain.

"Yes, this is the one thing left me now," he said with a sigh.

CHAPTER X

S oon after his admission to the Masonic Brotherhood, Pierre went to the Kiev province, where he had the greatest number of serfs, taking with him full directions which he had written down for his own guidance as to what he should do on his estates.

When he reached Kiev he sent for all his stewards to the head office and explained to them his intentions and wishes. He told them that steps would be taken immediately to free his serfs—and that till then they were not to be overburdened with labor, women while nursing their babies were not to be sent to work, assistance was to be given to the serfs, punishments were to be admonitory and not corporal, and hospitals, asylums, and schools were to be established on all the estates. Some of the stewards (there were semiliterate foremen among them) listened with alarm, supposing these words to mean that the young count was displeased with their management and embezzlement of money, some after their first fright were amused by Pierre's lisp and the new words they had not heard before, others simply enjoyed hearing how the master talked, while the cleverest among them, including the chief steward, understood from this speech how they could best handle the master for their own ends.

The chief steward expressed great sympathy with Pierre's intentions, but remarked that besides these changes it would be necessary to go into the general state of affairs which was far from satisfactory.

Despite Count Bezúkhov's enormous wealth, since he had come into an income which was said to amount to five hundred thousand rubles a year, Pierre felt himself far poorer than when his father had made him an allowance of ten thousand rubles. He had a dim perception of the following budget:

About 80,000 went in payments on all the estates to the Land Bank, about 30,000 went for the upkeep of the estate near Moscow, the town house, and the allowance to the three princesses; about 15,000 was given in pensions and the same amount for asylums; 150,000 alimony was sent to the countess; about 70,000 went for interest on debts. The building of a new church, previously begun, had cost about 10,000 in each of the last two years, and he did not know how the rest, about 100,000 rubles, was spent, and almost every year he was obliged to borrow. Besides this the chief steward wrote every year telling him of fires and bad harvests, or of the necessity of rebuilding factories and workshops. So the first task Pierre had to face was one for which he had very little aptitude or inclination—practical business.

He discussed estate affairs every day with his chief steward. But he felt that this did not forward matters at all. He felt that these consultations were detached from real affairs and did not link up with them or make them move. On the one hand, the chief steward put the state of things to him in the very worst light, pointing out the necessity of paying off the debts and undertaking new activities with serf labor, to which Pierre did not agree. On the other hand, Pierre demanded that steps should be taken to liberate the serfs, which the steward met by showing the necessity of first paying off the loans from the Land Bank, and the consequent impossibility of a speedy emancipation.

The steward did not say it was quite impossible, but suggested selling the forests in the province of Kostromá, the land lower down the river, and the Crimean estate, in order to make it possible: all of which operations according to him were connected with such complicated measures—the removal of injunctions, petitions, permits, and so on—that Pierre became quite bewildered and only replied:

"Yes, yes, do so."

Pierre had none of the practical persistence that would have enabled him to attend to the business himself and so he disliked it and only tried to pretend to the steward that he was attending to it. The steward for his part tried to pretend to the count that he considered these consultations very valuable for the proprietor and troublesome to himself.

In Kiev Pierre found some people he knew, and strangers hastened to make his acquaintance and joyfully welcomed the rich newcomer, the largest landowner of the province. Temptations to Pierre's greatest weakness—the one to which he had confessed when admitted to the Lodge—were so strong that he could not resist them. Again whole days, weeks, and months of his life passed in as great a rush and were as much occupied with evening parties, dinners, lunches, and balls, giving him no time for reflection, as in Petersburg. Instead of the new life he had hoped to lead he still lived the old life, only in new surroundings.

Of the three precepts of Freemasonry Pierre realized that he did not fulfill the one which enjoined every Mason to set an example of moral life, and that of the seven virtues he lacked two—morality and the love of death. He consoled himself with the thought that he fulfilled another of the precepts—that of reforming the human race—and had other virtues—love of his neighbor, and especially generosity.

In the spring of 1807 he decided to return to Petersburg. On the way he intended to visit all his estates and see for himself how far his orders had been carried out and in what state were the serfs whom God had entrusted to his care and whom he intended to benefit.

The chief steward, who considered the young count's attempts almost insane—unprofitable to himself, to the count, and to the serfs—made some concessions. Continuing to represent the liberation of the serfs as impracticable, he arranged for the erection of large buildings—schools, hospitals, and asylums—on all the estates before the master arrived. Everywhere preparations were made not for ceremonious welcomes (which he knew Pierre would not like), but for just such gratefully religious ones, with offerings of icons and the bread and salt of hospitality, as, according to his understanding of his master, would touch and delude him.

The southern spring, the comfortable rapid traveling in a Vienna carriage, and the solitude of the road, all had a gladdening effect on Pierre. The estates he had not before visited were each more picturesque than the other; the serfs everywhere seemed thriving and touchingly grateful for the benefits conferred on them. Everywhere were receptions, which though they embarrassed Pierre awakened a joyful feeling in the depth of his heart. In one place the peasants presented him with bread and salt and an icon of Saint Peter and Saint Paul, asking permission, as a mark of their gratitude for the benefits he had conferred on them, to build a new chantry to the church at their own expense in honor of Peter and Paul, his patron saints. In another place the women with infants in arms met him to thank him for releasing them from hard work. On a third estate the priest, bearing a cross, came to meet him surrounded by children whom, by the count's generosity, he was instructing in reading, writing, and religion. On all his estates Pierre saw with his own eyes brick buildings erected or in course of erection, all on one plan, for hospitals, schools, and almshouses, which were soon to be opened. Everywhere he saw the stewards' accounts, according to which the serfs' manorial labor had been diminished, and heard the touching thanks of deputations of serfs in their full-skirted blue coats.

What Pierre did not know was that the place where they presented him with bread and salt and wished to build a chantry in honor of Peter and Paul was a market village where a fair was held on St. Peter's day, and that the richest peasants (who formed the deputation) had begun the chantry long before, but that nine tenths of the peasants in that villages were in a state of the greatest poverty. He did not know that since the nursing mothers were no longer sent to work on his land, they did still harder work on their own land. He did not know that the priest who met him with the cross oppressed the peasants by his exactions, and that the pupils' parents wept at having to let him take their children and secured their release by heavy payments. He did not know that the brick buildings, built to plan, were being built by serfs whose manorial labor was thus increased, though lessened on paper. He did not know that where the steward had shown him in the accounts that the serfs' payments had been diminished by a third, their obligatory manorial work had been increased by a half. And so Pierre was delighted with his visit to his estates and quite recovered the philanthropic mood in which he had left Petersburg, and wrote enthusiastic letters to his "brother-instructor" as he called the Grand Master.

"How easy it is, how little effort it needs, to do so much good," thought Pierre, "and how little attention we pay to it!"

He was pleased at the gratitude he received, but felt abashed at receiving it. This gratitude reminded him of how much more he might do for these simple, kindly people.

The chief steward, a very stupid but cunning man who saw perfectly through the naïve and intelligent count and played with him as with a toy, seeing the effect these prearranged receptions had on Pierre, pressed him still harder with proofs of the impossibility and above all the uselessness of freeing the serfs, who were quite happy as it was.

Pierre in his secret soul agreed with the steward that it would be difficult to imagine happier people, and that God only knew what would happen to them when they were free, but he insisted, though reluctantly, on what he thought right. The steward promised to do all in his power to carry out the count's wishes, seeing clearly that not only would the count never be able to find out whether all measures had been taken for the sale of the land and forests and to release them from the Land Bank, but would probably never even inquire and would never know that the newly erected buildings were standing empty and that the serfs continued to give in money and work all that other people's serfs gave—that is to say, all that could be got out of them.

CHAPTER XI

Returning from his journey through South Russia in the happiest state of mind, Pierre carried out an intention he had long had of visiting his friend Bolkónski, whom he had not seen for two years.

Boguchárovo lay in a flat uninteresting part of the country among fields and forests of fir and birch, which were partly cut down. The house lay behind a newly dug pond filled with water to the brink and with banks still bare of grass. It was at the end of a village that stretched along the highroad in the midst of a young copse in which were a few fir trees.

The homestead consisted of a threshing floor, outhouses, stables, a bathhouse, a lodge, and a large brick house with semicircular façade still in course of construction. Round the house was a garden newly laid out. The fences and gates were new and solid; two fire pumps and a water cart, painted green, stood in a shed; the paths were straight, the bridges were strong and had handrails. Everything bore an impress of tidiness and good management. Some domestic serfs Pierre met, in reply to inquiries as to where the prince lived, pointed out a small newly built lodge close to the pond. Antón, a man who had looked after Prince Andrew in his boyhood, helped Pierre out of his carriage, said that the prince was at home, and showed him into a clean little anteroom.

Pierre was struck by the modesty of the small though clean house after the brilliant surroundings in which he had last met his friend in Petersburg.

He quickly entered the small reception room with its still-unplastered wooden walls redolent of pine, and would have gone farther, but Antón ran ahead on tiptoe and knocked at a door.

"Well, what is it?" came a sharp, unpleasant voice.

"A visitor," answered Antón.

"Ask him to wait," and the sound was heard of a chair being pushed back.

Pierre went with rapid steps to the door and suddenly came face to face with Prince Andrew, who came out frowning and looking old. Pierre embraced him and lifting his spectacles kissed his friend on the cheek and looked at him closely.

"Well, I did not expect you, I am very glad," said Prince Andrew.

Pierre said nothing; he looked fixedly at his friend with surprise. He was struck by the change in him. His words were kindly and there was a smile on his lips and face, but his eyes were dull and lifeless and in spite of his evident wish to do so he could not give them a joyous and glad sparkle. Prince Andrew had grown thinner, paler, and more manly-looking, but what amazed and estranged Pierre till he got used to it were his inertia and a wrinkle on his brow indicating prolonged concentration on some one thought.

As is usually the case with people meeting after a prolonged separation, it was long before their conversation could settle on anything. They put questions and gave brief replies about things they knew ought to be talked over at length. At last the conversation gradually settled on some of the topics at first lightly touched on: their past life, plans for the future, Pierre's journeys and occupations, the war, and so on. The preoccupation and despondency which Pierre had noticed in his friend's look was now still more clearly expressed in the smile with which he listened to Pierre, especially when he spoke with joyful animation of the past or the future. It was as if Prince Andrew would have liked to sympathize with what Pierre was saying, but could not. The latter began to feel that it was in bad taste to speak of his enthusiasms, dreams, and hopes of happiness or goodness, in Prince Andrew's presence. He was ashamed to express his new Masonic views, which had been particularly revived and strengthened by his late tour. He checked himself, fearing to seem naïve, yet he felt an irresistible desire to show his friend as soon as possible that he was now a quite different, and better, Pierre than he had been in Petersburg.

"I can't tell you how much I have lived through since then. I hardly know myself again."

"Yes, we have altered much, very much, since then," said Prince Andrew.

"Well, and you? What are your plans?"

"Plans!" repeated Prince Andrew ironically. "My plans?" he said, as if astonished at the word. "Well, you see, I'm building. I mean to settle here altogether next year...."

Pierre looked silently and searchingly into Prince Andrew's face, which had grown much older.

"No, I meant to ask..." Pierre began, but Prince Andrew interrupted him.

"But why talk of me?... Talk *to* me, yes, tell me about your travels and all you have been doing on your estates."

Pierre began describing what he had done on his estates, trying as far as possible to conceal his own part in the improvements that had been made. Prince Andrew several times prompted Pierre's story of what he had been doing, as though it were all an old-time story, and he listened not only without interest but even as if ashamed of what Pierre was telling him.

Pierre felt uncomfortable and even depressed in his friend's company and at last became silent.

"I'll tell you what, my dear fellow," said Prince Andrew, who evidently also felt depressed and constrained with his visitor, "I am only bivouacking here and have just come to look round. I am going back to my sister today. I will introduce you to her. But of course you know her already," he said, evidently trying to entertain a visitor with whom he now found nothing in common. "We will go after dinner. And would you now like to look round my place?"

They went out and walked about till dinnertime, talking of the political news and common acquaintances like people who do not know each other intimately. Prince Andrew spoke with some animation and interest only of the new homestead he was constructing and its buildings, but even here, while on the scaffolding, in the midst of a talk explaining the future arrangements of the house, he interrupted himself:

"However, this is not at all interesting. Let us have dinner, and then we'll set off."

At dinner, conversation turned on Pierre's marriage.

"I was very much surprised when I heard of it," said Prince Andrew.

Pierre blushed, as he always did when it was mentioned, and said hurriedly: "I will tell you some time how it all happened. But you know it is all over, and forever."

"Forever?" said Prince Andrew. "Nothing's forever."

"But you know how it all ended, don't you? You heard of the duel?"

"And so you had to go through that too!"

"One thing I thank God for is that I did not kill that man," said Pierre.

"Why so?" asked Prince Andrew. "To kill a vicious dog is a very good thing really."

"No, to kill a man is bad—wrong."

"Why is it wrong?" urged Prince Andrew. "It is not given to man to know what is right and what is wrong. Men always did and always will err, and in nothing more than in what they consider right and wrong."

"What does harm to another is wrong," said Pierre, feeling with pleasure that for the first time since his arrival Prince Andrew was roused, had begun to talk, and wanted to express what had brought him to his present state.

"And who has told you what is bad for another man?" he asked.

"Bad! Bad!" exclaimed Pierre. "We all know what is bad for ourselves."

"Yes, we know that, but the harm I am conscious of in myself is something I cannot inflict on others," said Prince Andrew, growing more and more animated and evidently wishing to express his new outlook to Pierre. He spoke in French. "I only know two very real evils in life: remorse and illness. The only good is the absence of those evils. To live for myself avoiding those two evils is my whole philosophy now."

"And love of one's neighbor, and self-sacrifice?" began Pierre. "No, I can't agree with you! To live only so as not to do evil and not to have to repent is not enough. I lived like that, I lived for myself and ruined my life. And only now when I am living, or at least trying" (Pierre's modesty made him correct himself) "to live for others, only now have I understood all the happiness of life. No, I shall not agree with you, and you do not really believe what you are saying." Prince Andrew looked silently at Pierre with an ironic smile.

"When you see my sister, Princess Mary, you'll get on with her," he said. "Perhaps you are right for yourself," he added after a short pause, "but everyone lives in his own way. You lived for yourself and say you nearly ruined your life and only found happiness when you began living for others. I experienced just the reverse. I lived for glory.—And after all what is glory? The same love of others, a desire to do something for them, a desire for their approval.—So I lived for others, and not almost, but quite, ruined my life. And I have become calmer since I began to live only for myself."

"But what do you mean by living only for yourself?" asked Pierre, growing excited. "What about your son, your sister, and your father?"

"But that's just the same as myself—they are not *others*," explained Prince Andrew. "The others, one's neighbors, *le prochain*, as you and Princess Mary call it, are the chief source of all error and evil. *Le prochain*—your Kiev peasants to whom you want to do good."

And he looked at Pierre with a mocking, challenging expression. He evidently wished to draw him on.

"You are joking," replied Pierre, growing more and more excited. "What error or evil can there be in my wishing to do good, and even doing a little—though I did very little and did it very badly? What evil can there be in it if unfortunate people, our serfs, people like ourselves, were growing up and dying with no idea of God and truth beyond ceremonies and meaningless prayers and are now instructed in a comforting belief in future life, retribution, recompense, and consolation? What evil and error are there in it, if people were dying of disease without help while material assistance could so easily be rendered, and I supplied them with a doctor, a hospital, and an asylum for the aged? And is it not a palpable, unquestionable good if a peasant, or a woman with a baby, has no rest day or night and I give them rest and leisure?" said Pierre, hurrying and lisping. "And I have done that though badly and to a small extent; but I have done something toward it and you cannot persuade me that it was not a good action, and more than that, you can't make me believe that you do not think so yourself. And the main thing is," he continued, "that I know, and know for certain, that the enjoyment of doing this good is the only sure happiness in life."

"Yes, if you put it like that it's quite a different matter," said Prince Andrew. "I build a house and lay out a garden, and you build hospitals. The one and the other may serve as a pastime. But what's right and what's good must be judged by one who knows all, but not by us. Well, you want an argument," he added, "come on then."

They rose from the table and sat down in the entrance porch which served as a veranda.

"Come, let's argue then," said Prince Andrew, "You talk of schools," he went on, crooking a finger, "education and so forth; that is, you want to raise him" (pointing to a peasant who passed by them taking off his cap) "from his animal condition and awaken in him spiritual needs, while it seems to me that animal happiness is the only happiness possible, and that is just what you want to deprive him of. I envy him, but you want to make him what I am, without giving him my means. Then you say, 'lighten his toil.' But as I see it, physical labor is as essential to him, as much a condition of his existence, as mental activity is to you or me. You can't help thinking. I go to bed after two in the morning, thoughts come and I can't sleep but toss about till dawn, because I think and can't help thinking, just as he can't help plowing and mowing; if he didn't, he would go to the drink shop or fall ill. Just as I could not stand his terrible physical labor but should die of it in a week, so he could not stand my physical idleness, but would grow fat and die. The third thing—what else was it you talked about?" and Prince Andrew crooked a third finger. "Ah, yes, hospitals, medicine. He has a fit, he is dying, and you come and bleed him and patch him up. He will drag about as a cripple, a burden to everybody, for another ten years. It would be far easier and simpler for him to die. Others are being born and there are plenty of them as it is. It would be different if you grudged losing a laborer— that's how I regard him—but you want to cure him from love of him. And he does not want that. And besides, what a notion that medicine ever cured anyone! Killed them, yes!" said he, frowning angrily and turning away from Pierre.

Prince Andrew expressed his ideas so clearly and distinctly that it was evident he had reflected on this subject more than once, and he spoke readily and rapidly like a man who has not talked for a long time. His glance became more animated as his conclusions became more hopeless.

"Oh, that is dreadful, dreadful!" said Pierre. "I don't understand how one can live with such ideas. I had such moments myself not long ago, in Moscow and when traveling, but at such times I collapsed so that I don't live at all—everything seems hateful to me... myself most of all. Then I don't eat, don't wash... and how is it with you?..."

"Why not wash? That is not cleanly," said Prince Andrew; "on the contrary one must try to make one's life as pleasant as possible. I'm alive, that is not my fault, so I must live out my life as best I can without hurting others."

"But with such ideas what motive have you for living? One would sit without moving, undertaking nothing...."

"Life as it is leaves one no peace. I should be thankful to do nothing, but here on the one hand the local nobility have done me the honor to choose me to be their marshal; it was all I could do to get out of it. They could not understand that I have not the necessary qualifications for it—the kind of good-natured, fussy shallowness necessary for the position. Then there's this house, which must be built in order to have a nook of one's own in which to be quiet. And now there's this recruiting."

"Why aren't you serving in the army?"

"After Austerlitz!" said Prince Andrew gloomily. "No, thank you very much! I have promised myself not to serve again in the active Russian army. And I won't—not even if Bonaparte were here at Smolénsk threatening Bald Hills—even then I wouldn't serve in the Russian army! Well, as I was saying," he continued, recovering his composure, "now there's this recruiting. My father is chief in command of the Third District, and my only way of avoiding active service is to serve under him."

"Then you are serving?"

"I am."

He paused a little while.

"And why do you serve?"

"Why, for this reason! My father is one of the most remarkable men of his time. But he is growing old, and though not exactly cruel he has too energetic a character. He is so accustomed to unlimited power that he is terrible, and now he has this authority of a commander in chief of the recruiting, granted by the Emperor. If I had been two hours late a fortnight ago he would have had a paymaster's clerk at Yúkhnovna hanged," said Prince Andrew with a smile. "So I am serving because I alone have any influence with my father, and now and then can save him from actions which would torment him afterwards."

"Well, there you see!"

"Yes, but it is not as you imagine," Prince Andrew continued. "I did not, and do not, in the least care about that scoundrel of a clerk who had stolen some boots from the recruits; I should even have been very glad to see him hanged, but I was sorry for my father—that again is for myself."

Prince Andrew grew more and more animated. His eyes glittered feverishly while he tried to prove to Pierre that in his actions there was no desire to do good to his neighbor.

"There now, you wish to liberate your serfs," he continued; "that is a very good thing, but not for you—I don't suppose you ever had anyone flogged or sent to Siberia—and still less for your serfs. If they are beaten, flogged, or sent to Siberia, I don't suppose they are any the worse off. In Siberia they lead the same animal life, and the stripes on their bodies heal, and they are happy as before. But it is a good thing for proprietors who perish morally, bring remorse upon themselves, stifle this remorse and grow callous, as a result of being able to inflict punishments justly and unjustly. It is those people I pity, and for their sake I should like to liberate the serfs. You may not have seen, but I have seen, how good men brought up in those traditions of unlimited power, in time when they grow more irritable, become cruel and harsh, are conscious of it, but cannot restrain themselves and grow more and more miserable."

Prince Andrew spoke so earnestly that Pierre could not help thinking that these thoughts had been suggested to Prince Andrew by his father's case.

He did not reply.

"So that's what I'm sorry for—human dignity, peace of mind, purity, and not the serfs' backs and foreheads, which, beat and shave as you may, always remain the same backs and foreheads."

"No, no! A thousand times no! I shall never agree with you," said Pierre.

CHAPTER XII

In the evening Andrew and Pierre got into the open carriage and drove to Bald Hills. Prince Andrew, glancing at Pierre, broke the silence now and then with remarks which showed that he was in a good temper.

Pointing to the fields, he spoke of the improvements he was making in his husbandry.

Pierre remained gloomily silent, answering in monosyllables and apparently immersed in his own thoughts.

He was thinking that Prince Andrew was unhappy, had gone astray, did not see the true light, and that he, Pierre, ought to aid, enlighten, and raise him. But as soon as he thought of what he should say, he felt that Prince Andrew with one word, one argument, would upset all his teaching, and he shrank from beginning, afraid of exposing to possible ridicule what to him was precious and sacred.

"No, but why do you think so?" Pierre suddenly began, lowering his head and looking like a bull about to charge, "why do you think so? You should not think so."

"Think? What about?" asked Prince Andrew with surprise.

"About life, about man's destiny. It can't be so. I myself thought like that, and do you know what saved me? Freemasonry! No, don't smile. Freemasonry is not a religious ceremonial sect, as I thought it was: Freemasonry is the best expression of the best, the eternal, aspects of humanity."

And he began to explain Freemasonry as he understood it to Prince Andrew. He said that Freemasonry is the teaching of

Christianity freed from the bonds of State and Church, a teaching of equality, brotherhood, and love.

"Only our holy brotherhood has the real meaning of life, all the rest is a dream," said Pierre. "Understand, my dear fellow, that outside this union all is filled with deceit and falsehood and I agree with you that nothing is left for an intelligent and good man but to live out his life, like you, merely trying not to harm others. But make our fundamental convictions your own, join our brotherhood, give yourself up to us, let yourself be guided, and you will at once feel yourself, as I have felt myself, a part of that vast invisible chain the beginning of which is hidden in heaven," said Pierre.

Prince Andrew, looking straight in front of him, listened in silence to Pierre's words. More than once, when the noise of the wheels prevented his catching what Pierre said, he asked him to repeat it, and by the peculiar glow that came into Prince Andrew's eyes and by his silence, Pierre saw that his words were not in vain and that Prince Andrew would not interrupt him or laugh at what he said.

They reached a river that had overflowed its banks and which they had to cross by ferry. While the carriage and horses were being placed on it, they also stepped on the raft.

Prince Andrew, leaning his arms on the raft railing, gazed silently at the flooding waters glittering in the setting sun.

"Well, what do you think about it?" Pierre asked. "Why are you silent?"

"What do I think about it? I am listening to you. It's all very well.... You say: join our brotherhood and we will show you the aim of life, the destiny of man, and the laws which govern the world. But who are *we?* Men. How is it you know everything? Why do I alone not see what you see? You see a reign of goodness and truth on earth, but I don't see it."

Pierre interrupted him.

"Do you believe in a future life?" he asked.

"A future life?" Prince Andrew repeated, but Pierre, giving him no time to reply, took the repetition for a denial, the more readily as he knew Prince Andrew's former atheistic convictions.

"You say you can't see a reign of goodness and truth on earth. Nor could I, and it cannot be seen if one looks on our life here as the end of everything. On *earth*, here on this earth" (Pierre pointed to the fields), "there is no truth, all is false and evil; but in the universe, in the whole universe there is a kingdom of truth, and we who are now the children of earth are—eternally—children of the whole universe. Don't I feel in my soul that I am part of this vast harmonious whole? Don't I feel that I form one link, one step, between the lower and higher beings, in this vast harmonious multitude of beings in whom the Deity—the Supreme Power if you prefer the term—is manifest? If I see, clearly see, that ladder leading from plant to man, why should I suppose it breaks off at me and does not go farther and farther? I feel that I cannot vanish, since nothing vanishes in this world, but that I shall always exist and always have existed. I feel that beyond me and above me there are spirits, and that in this world there is truth."

"Yes, that is Herder's theory," said Prince Andrew, "but it is not that which can convince me, dear friend—life and death are what convince. What convinces is when one sees a being dear to one, bound up with one's own life, before whom one was to blame and had hoped to make it right" (Prince Andrew's voice trembled and he turned away), "and suddenly that being is seized with pain, suffers, and ceases to exist.... Why? It cannot be that there is no answer. And I believe there is.... That's what convinces, that is what has convinced me," said Prince Andrew.

"Yes, yes, of course," said Pierre, "isn't that what I'm saying?"

"No. All I say is that it is not argument that convinces me of the necessity of a future life, but this: when you go hand in hand with someone and all at once that person vanishes *there, into nowhere*, and you yourself are left facing that abyss, and look in. And I have looked in...."

"Well, that's it then! You know that there is a *there* and there is a *Someone? There* is the future life. The *Someone* is—God."

Prince Andrew did not reply. The carriage and horses had long since been taken off, onto the farther bank, and reharnessed. The sun had sunk half below the horizon and an evening frost was starring the puddles near the ferry, but Pierre and Andrew, to the astonishment of the footmen, coachmen, and ferrymen, still stood on the raft and talked.

"If there is a God and future life, there is truth and good, and man's highest happiness consists in striving to attain them. We must live, we must love, and we must believe that we live not only today on this scrap of earth, but have lived and shall live forever, there, in the Whole," said Pierre, and he pointed to the sky.

Prince Andrew stood leaning on the railing of the raft listening to Pierre, and he gazed with his eyes fixed on the red reflection of the sun gleaming on the blue waters. There was perfect stillness. Pierre became silent. The raft had long since stopped and only the waves of the current beat softly against it below. Prince Andrew felt as if the sound of the waves kept up a refrain to Pierre's words, whispering:

"It is true, believe it."

He sighed, and glanced with a radiant, childlike, tender look at Pierre's face, flushed and rapturous, but yet shy before his superior friend.

"Yes, if it only were so!" said Prince Andrew. "However, it is time to get on," he added, and, stepping off the raft, he looked up at the sky to which Pierre had pointed, and for the first time since Austerlitz saw that high, everlasting sky he had seen while lying on that battlefield; and something that had long been slumbering, something that was best within him, suddenly awoke, joyful and youthful, in his soul. It vanished as soon as he returned to the customary conditions of his life, but he knew that this feeling which he did not know how to develop existed within him. His meeting with Pierre formed an epoch in Prince Andrew's life. Though outwardly he continued to live in the same old way, inwardly he began a new life.

CHAPTER XIII

It was getting dusk when Prince Andrew and Pierre drove up to the front entrance of the house at Bald Hills. As they approached the house, Prince Andrew with a smile drew Pierre's attention to a commotion going on at the back porch. A woman, bent with age, with a wallet on her back, and a short, long-haired, young man in a black garment had rushed back to the gate on seeing the carriage driving up. Two women ran out after them, and all four, looking round at the carriage, ran in dismay up the steps of the back porch.

"Those are Mary's 'God's folk,'" said Prince Andrew. "They have mistaken us for my father. This is the one matter in which she disobeys him. He orders these pilgrims to be driven away, but she receives them."

"But what are 'God's folk'?" asked Pierre.

Prince Andrew had no time to answer. The servants came out to meet them, and he asked where the old prince was and whether he was expected back soon.

The old prince had gone to the town and was expected back any minute.

Prince Andrew led Pierre to his own apartments, which were always kept in perfect order and readiness for him in his father's house; he himself went to the nursery.

"Let us go and see my sister," he said to Pierre when he returned. "I have not found her yet, she is hiding now, sitting with her 'God's folk.' It will serve her right, she will be confused, but you will see her 'God's folk.' It's really very curious."

"What are 'God's folk'?" asked Pierre.

"Come, and you'll see for yourself."

Princess Mary really was disconcerted and red patches came on her face when they went in. In her snug room, with lamps burning before the icon stand, a young lad with a long nose and long hair, wearing a monk's cassock, sat on the sofa beside her, behind a samovar. Near them, in an armchair, sat a thin, shriveled, old woman, with a meek expression on her childlike face.

"Andrew, why didn't you warn me?" said the princess, with mild reproach, as she stood before her pilgrims like a hen before her chickens.

"Charmée de vousvoir. Je suistrèscontente de vousvoir," * she said to Pierre as he kissed her hand. She had known him as a child, and now his friendship with Andrew, his misfortune with his wife, and above all his kindly, simple face disposed her favorably toward him. She looked at him with her beautiful radiant eyes and seemed to say, "I like you very much, but please don't laugh at my people." After exchanging the first greetings, they sat down.

* "Delighted to see you. I am very glad to see you."

"Ah, and Ivánushka is here too!" said Prince Andrew, glancing with a smile at the young pilgrim.

"Andrew!" said Princess Mary, imploringly. "Il faut que voussachiez que c'estune femme," * said Prince Andrew to Pierre.

"Andrew, au nom de Dieu!" *(2) Princess Mary repeated.

* "You must know that this is a woman."

* (2) "For heaven's sake."

It was evident that Prince Andrew's ironical tone toward the pilgrims and Princess Mary's helpless attempts to protect them were their customary long-established relations on the matter.

"Mais, ma bonne amie," said Prince Andrew, "vousdevriez au contraire m'êtrereconnaissante de ce que j'explique à Pierre votreintimité avec cejeune homme." *

---

* "But, my dear, you ought on the contrary to be grateful to me for explaining to Pierre your intimacy with this young man."

"Really?" said Pierre, gazing over his spectacles with curiosity and seriousness (for which Princess Mary was specially grateful to him) into Ivánushka's face, who, seeing that she was being spoken about, looked round at them all with crafty eyes.

Princess Mary's embarrassment on *her people's* account was quite unnecessary. They were not in the least abashed. The old woman, lowering her eyes but casting side glances at the newcomers, had turned her cup upside down and placed a nibbled bit of sugar beside it, and sat quietly in her armchair, though hoping to be offered another cup of tea. Ivánushka, sipping out of her saucer, looked with sly womanish eyes from under her brows at the young men.

"Where have you been? To Kiev?" Prince Andrew asked the old woman.

"I have, good sir," she answered garrulously. "Just at Christmastime I was deemed worthy to partake of the holy and heavenly sacrament at the shrine of the saint. And now I'm from Kolyázin, master, where a great and wonderful blessing has been revealed."

"And was Ivánushka with you?"

"I go by myself, benefactor," said Ivánushka, trying to speak in a bass voice. "I only came across Pelagéya in Yúkhnovo...."

Pelagéya interrupted her companion; she evidently wished to tell what she had seen.

"In Kolyázin, master, a wonderful blessing has been revealed."

"What is it? Some new relics?" asked Prince Andrew.

"Andrew, do leave off," said Princess Mary. "Don't tell him, Pelagéya."

"No... why not, my dear, why shouldn't I? I like him. He is kind, he is one of God's chosen, he's a benefactor, he once gave me ten rubles, I remember. When I was in Kiev, Crazy Cyril says to me (he's one of God's own and goes barefoot summer and winter), he says, 'Why are you not going to the right place? Go to Kolyázin where a wonder-working icon of the Holy Mother of God has been revealed.' On hearing those words I said good-by to the holy folk and went."

All were silent, only the pilgrim woman went on in measured tones, drawing in her breath.

"So I come, master, and the people say to me: 'A great blessing has been revealed, holy oil trickles from the cheeks of our blessed Mother, the Holy Virgin Mother of God.'..."

"All right, all right, you can tell us afterwards," said Princess Mary, flushing.

"Let me ask her," said Pierre. "Did you see it yourselves?" he inquired.

"Oh, yes, master, I was found worthy. Such a brightness on the face like the light of heaven, and from the blessed Mother's cheek it drops and drops...."

"But, dear me, that must be a fraud!" said Pierre, naïvely, who had listened attentively to the pilgrim.

"Oh, master, what are you saying?" exclaimed the horrified Pelagéya, turning to Princess Mary for support.

"They impose on the people," he repeated.

"Lord Jesus Christ!" exclaimed the pilgrim woman, crossing herself. "Oh, don't speak so, master! There was a general who did not believe, and said, 'The monks cheat,' and as soon as he'd said it he went blind. And he dreamed that the Holy Virgin Mother of the Kiev catacombs came to him and said, 'Believe in me and I will make you whole.' So he begged: 'Take me to her, take me to her.' It's the real truth I'm telling you, I saw it myself. So he was brought, quite blind, straight to her, and he goes up to her and falls down and says, 'Make me whole,' says he, 'and I'll give thee what the Tsar bestowed on me.' I saw it myself, master, the star is fixed into the icon. Well, and what do you think? He received his sight! It's a sin to speak so. God will punish you," she said admonishingly, turning to Pierre.

"How did the star get into the icon?" Pierre asked.

"And was the Holy Mother promoted to the rank of general?" said Prince Andrew, with a smile.

Pelagéya suddenly grew quite pale and clasped her hands.

"Oh, master, master, what a sin! And you who have a son!" she began, her pallor suddenly turning to a vivid red. "Master, what have you said? God forgive you!" And she crossed herself. "Lord forgive him! My dear, what does it mean?..." she asked, turning to Princess Mary. She got up and, almost crying, began to arrange her wallet. She evidently felt frightened and ashamed to have accepted charity in a house where such things could be said, and was at the same time sorry to have now to forgo the charity of this house.

"Now, why need you do it?" said Princess Mary. "Why did you come to me?..."

"Come, Pelagéya, I was joking," said Pierre. "*Princesse, ma parole, je n'ai pas voulu l'offenser. * I* did not mean anything, I was only joking," he said, smiling shyly and trying to efface his offense. "It was all my fault, and Andrew was only joking."

* "Princess, on my word, I did not wish to offend her."

Pelagéya stopped doubtfully, but in Pierre's face there was such a look of sincere penitence, and Prince Andrew glanced so meekly now at her and now at Pierre, that she was gradually reassured.

CHAPTER XIV

The pilgrim woman was appeased and, being encouraged to talk, gave a long account of Father Amphilochus, who led so holy a life that his hands smelled of incense, and how on her last visit to Kiev some monks she knew let her have the keys of the catacombs, and how she, taking some dried bread with her, had spent two days in the catacombs with the saints. "I'd pray awhile to one, ponder awhile, then go on to another. I'd sleep a bit and then again go and kiss the relics, and there was such peace all around, such blessedness, that one don't want to come out, even into the light of heaven again."

Pierre listened to her attentively and seriously. Prince Andrew went out of the room, and then, leaving "God's folk" to finish their tea, Princess Mary took Pierre into the drawing room.

"You are very kind," she said to him.

"Oh, I really did not mean to hurt her feelings. I understand them so well and have the greatest respect for them."

Princess Mary looked at him silently and smiled affectionately.

"I have known you a long time, you see, and am as fond of you as of a brother," she said. "How do you find Andrew?" she added hurriedly, not giving him time to reply to her affectionate words. "I am very anxious about him. His health was better in the winter, but last spring his wound reopened and the doctor said he ought to go away for a cure. And I am also very much afraid for him spiritually. He has not a character like us women who, when we suffer, can weep away our sorrows. He keeps it all within him. Today he is cheerful and in good spirits, but that is the effect of your visit—he is not often like that. If you could persuade him to go abroad. He needs activity, and this quiet regular life is very bad for him. Others don't notice it, but I see it."

Toward ten o'clock the men servants rushed to the front door, hearing the bells of the old prince's carriage approaching. Prince Andrew and Pierre also went out into the porch.

"Who's that?" asked the old prince, noticing Pierre as he got out of the carriage.

"Ah! Very glad! Kiss me," he said, having learned who the young stranger was.

The old prince was in a good temper and very gracious to Pierre.

Before supper, Prince Andrew, coming back to his father's study, found him disputing hotly with his visitor. Pierre was maintaining that a time would come when there would be no more wars. The old prince disputed it chaffingly, but without getting angry.

"Drain the blood from men's veins and put in water instead, then there will be no more war! Old women's nonsense—old women's nonsense!" he repeated, but still he patted Pierre affectionately on the shoulder, and then went up to the table where Prince Andrew, evidently not wishing to join in the conversation, was looking over the papers his father had brought from town. The old prince went up to him and began to talk business.

"The marshal, a Count Rostóv, hasn't sent half his contingent. He came to town and wanted to invite me to dinner—I gave him a pretty dinner!... And there, look at this.... Well, my boy," the old prince went on, addressing his son and patting Pierre on the shoulder. "A fine fellow—your friend—I like him! He stirs me up. Another says clever things and one doesn't care to listen, but this one talks rubbish yet stirs an old fellow up. Well, go! Get along! Perhaps I'll come and sit with you at supper. We'll have another dispute. Make friends with my little fool, Princess Mary," he shouted after Pierre, through the door.

Only now, on his visit to Bald Hills, did Pierre fully realize the strength and charm of his friendship with Prince Andrew. That charm was not expressed so much in his relations with him as with all his family and with the household. With the stern old prince and the gentle, timid Princess Mary, though he had scarcely known them, Pierre at once felt like an old friend. They were all fond of him already. Not only Princess Mary, who had been won by his gentleness with the pilgrims, gave him her most radiant looks, but even the one-year-old "Prince Nicholas" (as his grandfather called him) smiled at Pierre and let himself be taken in his arms, and Michael Ivánovich and Mademoiselle Bourienne looked at him with pleasant smiles when he talked to the old prince.

The old prince came in to supper; this was evidently on Pierre's account. And during the two days of the young man's visit he was extremely kind to him and told him to visit them again.

When Pierre had gone and the members of the household met together, they began to express their opinions of him as people always do after a new acquaintance has left, but as seldom happens, no one said anything but what was good of him.

CHAPTER XV

When returning from his leave, Rostóv felt, for the first time, how close was the bond that united him to Denísov and the whole regiment.

On approaching it, Rostóv felt as he had done when approaching his home in Moscow. When he saw the first hussar with the unbuttoned uniform of his regiment, when he recognized red-haired Deméntyev and saw the picket ropes of the roan horses, when Lavrúshka gleefully shouted to his master, "The count has come!" and Denísov, who had been asleep on his bed, ran all disheveled out of the mud hut to embrace him, and the officers collected round to greet the new arrival, Rostóv experienced the same feeling as when his mother, his father, and his sister had embraced him, and tears of joy choked him so that he could not speak. The regiment was also a home, and as unalterably dear and precious as his parents' house.

When he had reported himself to the commander of the regiment and had been reassigned to his former squadron, had been on duty and had gone out foraging, when he had again entered into all the little interests of the regiment and felt himself deprived of liberty and bound in one narrow, unchanging frame, he experienced the same sense of peace, of moral support, and the same sense of being at home here in his own place, as he had felt under the parental roof. But here was none of all that turmoil of the world at large, where he did not know his right place and took mistaken decisions; here was no Sónya with whom he ought, or ought not, to have an explanation; here was no possibility of going there or not going there; here there were not twenty-four hours in the day which could be spent in such a variety of ways; there was not that innumerable crowd of people of whom not one was nearer to him or farther from him than another; there were none of those uncertain and undefined money relations with his father, and nothing to recall that terrible loss to Dólokhov. Here, in the regiment, all was clear and simple. The whole world was divided into two unequal parts: one, our Pávlograd regiment; the other, all the rest. And the rest was no concern of his. In the regiment, everything was definite: who was lieutenant, who captain, who was a good fellow, who a bad one, and most of all, who was a comrade. The canteenkeeper gave one credit, one's pay came every four months, there was nothing to think out or decide, you had only to do nothing that was considered bad in the Pávlograd regiment and, when given an order, to do what was clearly, distinctly, and definitely ordered—and all would be well.

Having once more entered into the definite conditions of this regimental life, Rostóv felt the joy and relief a tired man feels on lying down to rest. Life in the regiment, during this campaign, was all the pleasanter for him, because, after his loss to Dólokhov (for which, in spite of all his family's efforts to console him, he could not forgive himself), he had made up his mind to atone for his fault by serving, not as he had done before, but really well, and by being a perfectly first-rate comrade and officer—in a word, a splendid man altogether, a thing which seemed so difficult out *in the world*, but so possible in the regiment.

After his losses, he had determined to pay back his debt to his parents in five years. He received ten thousand rubles a year, but now resolved to take only two thousand and leave the rest to repay the debt to his parents.

Our army, after repeated retreats and advances and battles at Pultúsk and Preussisch-Eylau, was concentrated near Bartenstein. It was awaiting the Emperor's arrival and the beginning of a new campaign.

The Pávlograd regiment, belonging to that part of the army which had served in the 1805 campaign, had been recruiting up to strength in Russia, and arrived too late to take part in the first actions of the campaign. It had been neither at Pultúsk nor at Preussisch-Eylau and, when it joined the army in the field in the second half of the campaign, was attached to Plátov's division.

Plátov's division was acting independently of the main army. Several times parts of the Pávlograd regiment had exchanged shots with the enemy, had taken prisoners, and once had even captured Marshal Oudinot's carriages. In April the Pávlograds were stationed immovably for some weeks near a totally ruined and deserted German village.

A thaw had set in, it was muddy and cold, the ice on the river broke, and the roads became impassable. For days neither provisions for the men nor fodder for the horses had been issued. As no transports could arrive, the men dispersed about the abandoned and deserted villages, searching for potatoes, but found few even of these.

Everything had been eaten up and the inhabitants had all fled— if any remained, they were worse than beggars and nothing more could be taken from them; even the soldiers, usually pitiless enough, instead of taking anything from them, often gave them the last of their rations.

The Pávlograd regiment had had only two men wounded in action, but had lost nearly half its men from hunger and sickness. In the hospitals, death was so certain that soldiers suffering from fever, or the swelling that came from bad food, preferred to remain on duty, and hardly able to drag their legs went to the front rather than to the hospitals. When spring came on, the soldiers found a plant just showing out of the ground that looked like asparagus, which, for some reason, they called "Máshka's sweet root." It was very bitter, but they wandered about the fields seeking it and dug it out with their sabers and ate it, though they were ordered not to do so, as it was a noxious plant. That spring a new disease broke out among the soldiers, a swelling of the arms, legs, and face, which the doctors attributed to eating this root. But in spite of all this, the soldiers of Denísov's squadron fed chiefly on "Máshka's sweet root," because it was the second week that the last of the biscuits were being doled out at the rate of half a pound a man and the last potatoes received had sprouted and frozen.

The horses also had been fed for a fortnight on straw from the thatched roofs and had become terribly thin, though still covered with tufts of felty winter hair.

Despite this destitution, the soldiers and officers went on living just as usual. Despite their pale swollen faces and tattered uniforms, the hussars formed line for roll call, kept things in order, groomed their horses, polished their arms, brought in straw from the thatched roofs in place of fodder, and sat down to dine round the caldrons from which they rose up hungry, joking about their nasty food and their hunger. As usual, in their spare time, they lit bonfires, steamed themselves before them naked; smoked, picked out and baked sprouting rotten potatoes, told and listened to stories of Potëmkin's and Suvórov's campaigns, or to legends of Alësha the Sly, or the priest's laborerMikólka.

The officers, as usual, lived in twos and threes in the roofless, half-ruined houses. The seniors tried to collect straw and potatoes and, in general, food for the men. The younger ones occupied themselves as before, some playing cards (there was plenty of money, though there was no food), some with more innocent games, such as quoits and skittles. The general trend of the campaign was rarely spoken of, partly because nothing certain was known about it, partly because there was a vague feeling that in the main it was going badly.

Rostóv lived, as before, with Denísov, and since their furlough they had become more friendly than ever. Denísov never spoke of Rostóv's family, but by the tender friendship his commander showed him, Rostóv felt that the elder hussar's luckless love for Natásha played a part in strengthening their friendship. Denísov evidently tried to expose Rostóv to danger as seldom as possible, and after an action greeted his safe return with evident joy. On one of his foraging expeditions, in a deserted and ruined village to which he had come in search of provisions, Rostóv found a family consisting of an old Pole and his daughter with an infant in arms. They were half clad, hungry, too weak to get away on foot and had no means of obtaining a conveyance. Rostóv brought them to his quarters, placed them in his own lodging, and kept them for some weeks while the old man was recovering. One of his comrades, talking of women, began chaffing Rostóv, saying that he was more wily than any of them and that it would not be a bad thing if he introduced to them the pretty Polish girl he had saved. Rostóv took the joke as an insult, flared up, and said such unpleasant things to the officer that it was all Denísovcould do to prevent a duel. When the officer had gone away, Denísov, who did not himself know what Rostóv's relations with the Polish girl might be, began to upbraid him for his quickness of temper, and Rostóv replied:

"Say what you like.... She is like a sister to me, and I can't tell you how it offended me... because... well, for that reason...."

Denísov patted him on the shoulder and began rapidly pacing the room without looking at Rostóv, as was his way at moments of deep feeling.

"Ah, what a mad bweed you Wostóvs are!" he muttered, and Rostóv noticed tears in his eyes.

CHAPTER XVI

In April the troops were enlivened by news of the Emperor's arrival, but Rostóv had no chance of being present at the review he held at Bartenstein, as the Pávlograds were at the outposts far beyond that place.

They were bivouacking. Denísov and Rostóv were living in an earth hut, dug out for them by the soldiers and roofed with branches and turf. The hut was made in the following manner, which had then come into vogue. A trench was dug three and a half feet wide, four feet eight inches deep, and eight feet long. At one end of the trench, steps were cut out and these formed the entrance and vestibule. The trench itself was the room, in which the lucky ones, such as the squadron commander, had a board, lying on piles at the end opposite the entrance, to serve as a table. On each side of the trench, the earth was cut out to a breadth of about two and a half feet, and this did duty for bedsteads and couches. The roof was so constructed that one could stand up in the middle of the trench and could even sit up on the beds if one drew close to the table. Denísov, who was living luxuriously because the soldiers of his squadron liked him, had also a board in the roof at the farther end, with a piece of (broken but mended) glass in it for a window. When it was very cold, embers from the soldiers' campfire were placed on a bent sheet of iron on the steps in the "reception room"—as Denísov called that part of the hut—and it was then so warm that the officers, of whom there were always some with Denísov and Rostóv, sat in their shirt sleeves.

In April, Rostóv was on orderly duty. One morning, between seven and eight, returning after a sleepless night, he sent for embers, changed his rain-soaked underclothes, said his prayers, drank tea, got warm, then tidied up the things on the table and in his own corner, and, his face glowing from exposure to the wind and with nothing on but his shirt, lay down on his back, putting his arms under his head. He was pleasantly considering the probability of being promoted in a few days for his last reconnoitering expedition, and was awaiting Denísov, who had gone out somewhere and with whom he wanted a talk.

Suddenly he heard Denísov shouting in a vibrating voice behind the hut, evidently much excited. Rostóv moved to the window to see whom he was speaking to, and saw the quartermaster, Topchéenko.

"I ordered you not to let them eat that Máshka woot stuff!" Denísov was shouting. "And I saw with my own eyes how Lazarchúkbwought some fwom the fields."

"I have given the order again and again, your honor, but they don't obey," answered the quartermaster.

Rostóv lay down again on his bed and thought complacently: "Let him fuss and bustle now, my job's done and I'm lying down—capitally!" He could hear that Lavrúshka—that sly, bold orderly of Denísov's—was talking, as well as the quartermaster. Lavrúshka was saying something about loaded wagons, biscuits, and oxen he had seen when he had gone out for provisions.

Then Denísov's voice was heard shouting farther and farther away. "Saddle! Second platoon!"

"Where are they off to now?" thought Rostóv.

Five minutes later, Denísov came into the hut, climbed with muddy boots on the bed, lit his pipe, furiously scattered his things about, took his leaded whip, buckled on his saber, and went out again. In answer to Rostóv's inquiry where he was going, he answered vaguely and crossly that he had some business.

"Let God and our gweat monarch judge me afterwards!" said Denísov going out, and Rostóv heard the hoofs of several horses splashing through the mud. He did not even trouble to find out where Denísov had gone. Having got warm in his corner, he fell asleep and did not leave the hut till toward evening. Denísov had not yet returned. The weather had cleared up, and near the next hut two officers and a cadet were playing *sváyka*, laughing as they threw their missiles which buried themselves in the soft mud. Rostóv joined them. In the middle of the game, the officers saw some wagons approaching with fifteen hussars on their skinny horses behind them. The wagons escorted by the hussars drew up to the picket ropes and a crowd of hussars surrounded them.

"There now, Denísov has been worrying," said Rostóv, "and here are the provisions."

"So they are!" said the officers. "Won't the soldiers be glad!"

A little behind the hussars came Denísov, accompanied by two infantry officers with whom he was talking.

Rostóv went to meet them.

"I warn you, Captain," one of the officers, a short thin man, evidently very angry, was saying.

"Haven't I told you I won't give them up?" replied Denísov.

"You will answer for it, Captain. It is mutiny—seizing the transport of one's own army. Our men have had nothing to eat for two days."

"And mine have had nothing for two weeks," said Denísov.

"It is robbery! You'll answer for it, sir!" said the infantry officer, raising his voice.

"Now, what are you pestewing me for?" cried Denísov, suddenly losing his temper. "I shall answer for it and not you, and you'd better not buzz about here till you get hurt. Be off! Go!" he shouted at the officers.

"Very well, then!" shouted the little officer, undaunted and not riding away. "If you are determined to rob, I'll..."

"Go to the devil! quick ma'ch, while you're safe and sound!" and Denísov turned his horse on the officer.

"Very well, very well!" muttered the officer, threateningly, and turning his horse he trotted away, jolting in his saddle.

"A dog astwide a fence! A weal dog astwide a fence!" shouted Denísov after him (the most insulting expression a cavalryman can address to a mounted infantryman) and riding up to Rostóv, he burst out laughing.

"I've taken twansports from the infantwy by force!" he said. "After all, can't let our men starve."

The wagons that had reached the hussars had been consigned to an infantry regiment, but learning from Lavrúshka that the transport was unescorted, Denísov with his hussars had seized it by force. The soldiers had biscuits dealt out to them freely, and they even shared them with the other squadrons.

The next day the regimental commander sent for Denísov, and holding his fingers spread out before his eyes said:

"This is how I look at this affair: I know nothing about it and won't begin proceedings, but I advise you to ride over to the staff and settle the business there in the commissariat department and if possible sign a receipt for such and such stores received. If not, as the demand was booked against an infantry regiment, there will be a row and the affair may end badly."

From the regimental commander's, Denísov rode straight to the staff with a sincere desire to act on this advice. In the evening he came back to his dugout in a state such as Rostóv had never yet seen him in. Denísov could not speak and gasped for breath. When Rostóv asked what was the matter, he only uttered some incoherent oaths and threats in a hoarse, feeble voice.

Alarmed at Denísov's condition, Rostóv suggested that he should undress, drink some water, and send for the doctor.

"Twy me for wobbewy... oh! Some more water... Let them twy me, but I'll always thwashscoundwels... and I'll tell the Empewo'... Ice..." he muttered.

The regimental doctor, when he came, said it was absolutely necessary to bleed Denísov. A deep saucer of black blood was taken from his hairy arm and only then was he able to relate what had happened to him.

"I get there," began Denísov. "'Now then, where's your chief's quarters?' They were pointed out. 'Please to wait.' 'I've widden twenty miles and have duties to attend to and no time to wait. Announce me.' Vewy well, so out comes their head chief—also took it into his head to lecture me: 'It's wobbewy!'—'Wobbewy,' I say, 'is not done by man who seizes pwovisions to feed his soldiers, but by him who takes them to fill his own pockets!' 'Will you please be silent?' 'Vewy good!' Then he says: 'Go and give a weceipt to the commissioner, but your affair will be passed on to headquarters.' I go to the commissioner. I enter, and at the table... who do you think? No, but wait a bit!... Who is it that's starving us?" shouted Denísov, hitting the table with the fist of his newly bled arm so violently that the table nearly broke down and the tumblers on it jumped about. "Telyánin! 'What? So it's you who's starving us to death! Is it? Take this and this!' and I hit him so pat, stwaight on his snout... 'Ah, what a... what a...!' and I sta'tedfwashing him... Well, I've had a bit of fun I can tell you!" cried Denísov, gleeful and yet angry, his white teeth showing under his black mustache. "I'd have killed him if they hadn't taken him away!"

"But what are you shouting for? Calm yourself," said Rostóv. "You've set your arm bleeding afresh. Wait, we must tie it up again."

Denísov was bandaged up again and put to bed. Next day he woke calm and cheerful.

But at noon the adjutant of the regiment came into Rostóv's and Denísov's dugout with a grave and serious face and regretfully showed them a paper addressed to Major Denísov from the regimental commander in which inquiries were made about yesterday's occurrence. The adjutant told them that the affair was likely to take a very bad turn: that a court-martial had been appointed, and that in view of the severity with which marauding and insubordination were now regarded, degradation to the ranks would be the best that could be hoped for.

The case, as represented by the offended parties, was that, after seizing the transports, Major Denísov, being drunk, went to the chief quartermaster and without any provocation called him a thief, threatened to strike him, and on being led out had rushed into the office and given two officials a thrashing, and dislocated the arm of one of them.

In answer to Rostóv's renewed questions, Denísov said, laughing, that he thought he remembered that some other fellow had got mixed up in it, but that it was all nonsense and rubbish, and he did not in the least fear any kind of trial, and that if those scoundrels dared attack him he would give them an answer that they would not easily forget.

Denísov spoke contemptuously of the whole matter, but Rostóv knew him too well not to detect that (while hiding it from others) at heart he feared a court-martial and was worried over the affair, which was evidently taking a bad turn. Every day, letters of inquiry and notices from the court arrived, and on the first of May, Denísov was ordered to hand the squadron over to the next in seniority and appear before the staff of his division to explain his violence at the commissariat office. On the previous day Plátovreconnoitered with two Cossack regiments and two squadrons of hussars. Denísov, as was his wont, rode out in front of the outposts, parading his courage. A bullet fired by a French sharpshooter hit him in the fleshy part of his leg. Perhaps at another time Denísov would not have left the regiment for so slight a wound, but now he took advantage of it to excuse himself from appearing at the staff and went into hospital.

CHAPTER XVII

I n June the battle of Friedland was fought, in which the Pávlograds did not take part, and after that an armistice was proclaimed. Rostóv, who felt his friend's absence very much, having no news of him since he left and feeling very anxious about his wound and the progress of his affairs, took advantage of the armistice to get leave to visit Denísov in hospital.

The hospital was in a small Prussian town that had been twice devastated by Russian and French troops. Because it was summer, when it is so beautiful out in the fields, the little town presented a particularly dismal appearance with its broken roofs and fences, its foul streets, tattered inhabitants, and the sick and drunken soldiers wandering about.

The hospital was in a brick building with some of the window frames and panes broken and a courtyard surrounded by the remains of a wooden fence that had been pulled to pieces. Several bandaged soldiers, with pale swollen faces, were sitting or walking about in the sunshine in the yard.

Directly Rostóv entered the door he was enveloped by a smell of putrefaction and hospital air. On the stairs he met a Russian army doctor smoking a cigar. The doctor was followed by a Russian assistant.

"I can't tear myself to pieces," the doctor was saying. "Come to MakárAlexéevich in the evening. I shall be there."

The assistant asked some further questions.

"Oh, do the best you can! Isn't it all the same?" The doctor noticed Rostóv coming upstairs.

"What do you want, sir?" said the doctor. "What do you want? The bullets having spared you, do you want to try typhus? This is a pesthouse, sir."

"How so?" asked Rostóv.

"Typhus, sir. It's death to go in. Only we two, Makéev and I" (he pointed to the assistant), "keep on here. Some five of us doctors have died in this place.... When a new one comes he is done for in a week," said the doctor with evident satisfaction. "Prussian doctors have been invited here, but our allies don't like it at all."

Rostóv explained that he wanted to see Major Denísov of the hussars, who was wounded.

"I don't know. I can't tell you, sir. Only think! I am alone in charge of three hospitals with more than four hundred patients! It's well that the charitable Prussian ladies send us two pounds of coffee and some lint each month or we should be lost!" he laughed. "Four hundred, sir, and they're always sending me fresh ones. There *are* four hundred? Eh?" he asked, turning to the assistant.

The assistant looked fagged out. He was evidently vexed and impatient for the talkative doctor to go.

"Major Denísov," Rostóv said again. "He was wounded at Molliten."

"Dead, I fancy. Eh, Makéev?" queried the doctor, in a tone of indifference.

The assistant, however, did not confirm the doctor's words.

"Is he tall and with reddish hair?" asked the doctor.

Rostóv described Denísov's appearance.

"There was one like that," said the doctor, as if pleased. "That one is dead, I fancy. However, I'll look up our list. We had a list. Have you got it, Makéev?"

"MakárAlexéevich has the list," answered the assistant. "But if you'll step into the officers' wards you'll see for yourself," he added, turning to Rostóv.

"Ah, you'd better not go, sir," said the doctor, "or you may have to stay here yourself."

But Rostóv bowed himself away from the doctor and asked the assistant to show him the way.

"Only don't blame me!" the doctor shouted up after him.

Rostóv and the assistant went into the dark corridor. The smell was so strong there that Rostóv held his nose and had to pause and collect his strength before he could go on. A door opened to the right, and an emaciated sallow man on crutches, barefoot and in underclothing, limped out and, leaning against the doorpost, looked with glittering envious eyes at those who were passing. Glancing in at the door, Rostóv saw that the sick and wounded were lying on the floor on straw and overcoats.

"May I go in and look?"

"What is there to see?" said the assistant.

But, just because the assistant evidently did not want him to go in, Rostóv entered the soldiers' ward. The foul air, to which he had already begun to get used in the corridor, was still stronger here. It was a little different, more pungent, and one felt that this was where it originated.

In the long room, brightly lit up by the sun through the large windows, the sick and wounded lay in two rows with their heads to the walls, and leaving a passage in the middle. Most of them were unconscious and paid no attention to the newcomers. Those who were conscious raised themselves or lifted their thin yellow faces, and all looked intently at Rostóv with the same expression of hope, of relief, reproach, and envy of another's health. Rostóv went to the middle of the room and looking through the open doors into the two adjoining rooms saw the same thing there. He stood still, looking silently around. He had not at all expected such a sight. Just before him, almost across the middle of the passage on the bare floor, lay a sick man, probably a Cossack to judge by the cut of his hair. The man lay on his back, his huge arms and legs outstretched. His face was purple, his eyes were rolled back so that only the whites were seen, and on his bare legs and arms which were still red, the veins stood out like cords. He was knocking the back of his head against the floor, hoarsely uttering some word which he kept repeating. Rostóv listened and made out the word. It was "drink, drink, a drink!" Rostóv glanced round, looking for someone who would put this man back in his place and bring him water.

"Who looks after the sick here?" he asked the assistant.

Just then a commissariat soldier, a hospital orderly, came in from the next room, marching stiffly, and drew up in front of Rostóv.

"Good day, your honor!" he shouted, rolling his eyes at Rostóv and evidently mistaking him for one of the hospital authorities.

"Get him to his place and give him some water," said Rostóv, pointing to the Cossack.

"Yes, your honor," the soldier replied complacently, and rolling his eyes more than ever he drew himself up still straighter, but did not move.

"No, it's impossible to do anything here," thought Rostóv, lowering his eyes, and he was going out, but became aware of an intense look fixed on him on his right, and he turned. Close to the corner, on an overcoat, sat an old, unshaven, gray-bearded soldier as thin as a skeleton, with a stern sallow face and eyes intently fixed on Rostóv. The man's neighbor on one side whispered something to him, pointing at Rostóv, who noticed that the old man wanted to speak to him. He drew nearer and saw that the old man had only one leg bent under him, the other had been amputated above the knee. His neighbor on the other side, who lay motionless some distance from him with his head thrown back, was a young soldier with a snub nose. His pale waxen face was still freckled and his eyes were rolled back. Rostóv looked at the young soldier and a cold chill ran down his back.

"Why, this one seems..." he began, turning to the assistant.

"And how we've been begging, your honor," said the old soldier, his jaw quivering. "He's been dead since morning. After all we're men, not dogs."

"I'll send someone at once. He shall be taken away—taken away at once," said the assistant hurriedly. "Let us go, your honor."

"Yes, yes, let us go," said Rostóv hastily, and lowering his eyes and shrinking, he tried to pass unnoticed between the rows of reproachful envious eyes that were fixed upon him, and went out of the room.

CHAPTER XVIII

Going along the corridor, the assistant led Rostóv to the officers' wards, consisting of three rooms, the doors of which stood open. There were beds in these rooms and the sick and wounded officers were lying or sitting on them. Some were walking about the rooms in hospital dressing gowns. The first person Rostóv met in the officers' ward was a thin little man with one arm, who was walking about the first room in a nightcap and hospital dressing gown, with a pipe between his teeth. Rostóv looked at him, trying to remember where he had seen him before.

"See where we've met again!" said the little man. "Túshin, Túshin, don't you remember, who gave you a lift at Schön Grabern? And I've had a bit cut off, you see..." he went on with a smile, pointing to the empty sleeve of his dressing gown. "Looking for VasíliDmítrichDenísov? My neighbor," he added, when he heard who Rostóv wanted. "Here, here," and Túshin led him into the next room, from whence came sounds of several laughing voices.

"How can they laugh, or even live at all here?" thought Rostóv, still aware of that smell of decomposing flesh that had been so strong in the soldiers' ward, and still seeming to see fixed on him those envious looks which had followed him out from both sides, and the face of that young soldier with eyes rolled back.

Denísov lay asleep on his bed with his head under the blanket, though it was nearly noon.

"Ah, Wostóv? How are you, how are you?" he called out, still in the same voice as in the regiment, but Rostóv noticed sadly that under this habitual ease and animation some new, sinister, hidden feeling showed itself in the expression of Denísov's face and the intonations of his voice.

His wound, though a slight one, had not yet healed even now, six weeks after he had been hit. His face had the same swollen pallor as the faces of the other hospital patients, but it was not this that struck Rostóv. What struck him was that Denísov did not seem glad to see him, and smiled at him unnaturally. He did not ask about the regiment, nor about the general state of affairs, and when Rostóv spoke of these matters did not listen.

Rostóv even noticed that Denísov did not like to be reminded of the regiment, or in general of that other free life which was going on outside the hospital. He seemed to try to forget that old life and was only interested in the affair with the commissariat officers. On Rostóv's inquiry as to how the matter stood, he at once produced from under his pillow a paper he had received from the commission and the rough draft of his answer to it. He became animated when he began reading his paper and specially drew Rostóv's attention to the stinging rejoinders he made to his enemies. His hospital companions, who had gathered round Rostóv—a fresh arrival from the world outside—gradually began to disperse as soon as Denísov began reading his answer. Rostóv noticed by their faces that all those gentlemen had already heard that story more than once and were tired of it. Only the man who had the next bed, a stout Uhlan, continued to sit on his bed, gloomily frowning and smoking a pipe, and little one-armed Túshin still listened, shaking his head disapprovingly. In the middle of the reading, the Uhlan interrupted Denísov.

"But what I say is," he said, turning to Rostóv, "it would be best simply to petition the Emperor for pardon. They say great rewards will now be distributed, and surely a pardon would be granted...."

"Me petition the Empewo'!" exclaimed Denísov, in a voice to which he tried hard to give the old energy and fire, but which sounded like an expression of irritable impotence. "What for? If I were a wobber I would ask mercy, but I'm being court-martialed for bwingingwobbers to book. Let them twy me, I'm not afwaid of anyone. I've served the Tsar and my countwyhonowably and have not stolen! And am I to be degwaded?... Listen, I'm w'iting to them stwaight. This is what I say: 'If I had wobbed the Tweasuwy...'"

"It's certainly well written," said Túshin, "but that's not the point, VasíliDmítrich," and he also turned to Rostóv. "One has to submit, and VasíliDmítrich doesn't want to. You know the auditor told you it was a bad business."

"Well, let it be bad," said Denísov.

"The auditor wrote out a petition for you," continued Túshin, "and you ought to sign it and ask this gentleman to take it. No doubt he" (indicating Rostóv) "has connections on the staff. You won't find a better opportunity."

"Haven't I said I'm not going to gwovel?" Denísov interrupted him, went on reading his paper.

Rostóv had not the courage to persuade Denísov, though he instinctively felt that the way advised by Túshin and the other officers was the safest, and though he would have been glad to be of service to Denísov. He knew his stubborn will and straightforward hasty temper.

When the reading of Denísov's virulent reply, which took more than an hour, was over, Rostóv said nothing, and he spent the rest of the day in a most dejected state of mind amid Denísov's hospital comrades, who had gathered round him, telling them what he knew and listening to their stories. Denísov was moodily silent all the evening.

Late in the evening, when Rostóv was about to leave, he asked Denísov whether he had no commission for him.

"Yes, wait a bit," said Denísov, glancing round at the officers, and taking his papers from under his pillow he went to the window, where he had an inkpot, and sat down to write.

"It seems it's no use knocking one's head against a wall!" he said, coming from the window and giving Rostóv a large envelope. In it was the petition to the Emperor drawn up by the auditor, in which Denísov, without alluding to the offenses of the commissariat officials, simply asked for pardon.

"Hand it in. It seems..."

He did not finish, but gave a painfully unnatural smile.

CHAPTER XIX

Having returned to the regiment and told the commander the state of Denísov's affairs, Rostóv rode to Tilsit with the letter to the Emperor.

On the thirteenth of June the French and Russian Emperors arrived in Tilsit. BorísDrubetskóy had asked the important personage on whom he was in attendance, to include him in the suite appointed for the stay at Tilsit.

"I should like to see the great man," he said, alluding to Napoleon, whom hitherto he, like everyone else, had always called Buonaparte.

"You are speaking of Buonaparte?" asked the general, smiling.

Borís looked at his general inquiringly and immediately saw that he was being tested.

"I am speaking, Prince, of the Emperor Napoleon," he replied. The general patted him on the shoulder, with a smile.

"You will go far," he said, and took him to Tilsit with him.

Borís was among the few present at the Niemen on the day the two Emperors met. He saw the raft, decorated with monograms, saw Napoleon pass before the French Guards on the farther bank of the river, saw the pensive face of the Emperor Alexander as he sat in silence in a tavern on the bank of the Niemen awaiting Napoleon's arrival, saw both Emperors get into boats, and saw how Napoleon—reaching the raft first—stepped quickly forward to meet Alexander and held out his hand to him, and how they both retired into the pavilion. Since he had begun to move in the highest circles Borís had made it his habit to watch attentively all that went on around him and to note it down. At the time of the meeting at Tilsit he asked the names of those who had come with Napoleon and about the uniforms they wore, and listened attentively to words spoken by important personages. At the moment the Emperors went into the pavilion he looked at his watch, and did not forget to look at it again when Alexander came out. The interview had lasted an hour and fifty-three minutes. He noted this down that same evening, among other facts he felt to be of historic importance. As the Emperor's suite was a very small one, it was a matter of great importance, for a man who valued his success in the service, to be at Tilsit on the occasion of this interview between the two Emperors, and having succeeded in this, Borís felt that henceforth his position was fully assured. He had not only become known, but people had grown accustomed to him and accepted him. Twice he had executed commissions to the Emperor himself, so that the latter knew his face, and all those at court, far from cold-shouldering him as at first when they considered him a newcomer, would now have been surprised had he been absent.

Borís lodged with another adjutant, the Polish Count Zhilínski. Zhilínski, a Pole brought up in Paris, was rich, and passionately fond of the French, and almost every day of the stay at Tilsit, French officers of the Guard and from French headquarters were dining and lunching with him and Borís.

On the evening of the twenty-fourth of June, Count Zhilínski arranged a supper for his French friends. The guest of honor was an aide-de-camp of Napoleon's, there were also several French officers of the Guard, and a page of Napoleon's, a young lad of an old aristocratic French family. That same day, Rostóv, profiting by the darkness to avoid being recognized in civilian dress, came to Tilsit and went to the lodging occupied by Borís and Zhilínski.

Rostóv, in common with the whole army from which he came, was far from having experienced the change of feeling toward Napoleon and the French—who from being foes had suddenly become friends—that had taken place at headquarters and in Borís. In the army, Bonaparte and the French were still regarded with mingled feelings of anger, contempt, and fear. Only recently, talking with one of Plátov's Cossack officers, Rostóv had argued that if Napoleon were taken prisoner he would be treated not as a sovereign, but as a criminal. Quite lately, happening to meet a wounded French colonel on the road, Rostóv had maintained with heat that peace was impossible between a legitimate sovereign and the criminal Bonaparte. Rostóv was therefore unpleasantly struck by the presence of French officers in Borís' lodging, dressed in uniforms he had been accustomed to see from quite a different point of view from the outposts of the flank. As soon as he noticed a French officer, who thrust his head out of the door, that warlike feeling of hostility which he always experienced at the sight of the enemy suddenly seized him. He stopped at the threshold and asked in Russian whether Drubetskóy lived there. Borís, hearing a strange voice in the anteroom, came out to meet him. An expression of annoyance showed itself for a moment on his face on first recognizing Rostóv.

"Ah, it's you? Very glad, very glad to see you," he said, however, coming toward him with a smile. But Rostóv had noticed his first impulse.

"I've come at a bad time I think. I should not have come, but I have business," he said coldly.

"No, I only wonder how you managed to get away from your regiment. *Dans un moment je suis à vous,*" * he said, answering someone who called him.

* "In a minute I shall be at your disposal."

"I see I'm intruding," Rostóv repeated.

The look of annoyance had already disappeared from Borís' face: having evidently reflected and decided how to act, he very quietly took both Rostóv's hands and led him into the next room. His eyes, looking serenely and steadily at Rostóv, seemed to be veiled by something, as if screened by blue spectacles of conventionality. So it seemed to Rostóv.

"Oh, come now! As if you could come at a wrong time!" said Borís, and he led him into the room where the supper table was laid and introduced him to his guests, explaining that he was not a civilian, but an hussar officer, and an old friend of his.

"Count Zhilínski—*le Comte* N. N.—*le Capitaine* S. S.," said he, naming his guests. Rostóv looked frowningly at the Frenchmen, bowed reluctantly, and remained silent.

Zhilínski evidently did not receive this new Russian person very willingly into his circle and did not speak to Rostóv. Borís did not appear to notice the constraint the newcomer produced and, with the same pleasant composure and the same veiled look in his eyes with which he had met Rostóv, tried to enliven the conversation. One of the Frenchmen, with the politeness characteristic of his countrymen, addressed the obstinately taciturn Rostóv, saying that the latter had probably come to Tilsit to see the Emperor.

"No, I came on business," replied Rostóv, briefly.

Rostóv had been out of humor from the moment he noticed the look of dissatisfaction on Borís' face, and as always happens to those in a bad humor, it seemed to him that everyone regarded him with aversion and that he was in everybody's way. He really was in their way, for he alone took no part in the conversation which again became general. The looks the visitors cast on him seemed to say: "And what is he sitting here for?" He rose and went up to Borís.

"Anyhow, I'm in your way," he said in a low tone. "Come and talk over my business and I'll go away."

"Oh, no, not at all," said Borís. "But if you are tired, come and lie down in my room and have a rest."

"Yes, really..."

They went into the little room where Borís slept. Rostóv, without sitting down, began at once, irritably (as if Borís were to blame in some way) telling him about Denísov's affair, asking him whether, through his general, he could and would intercede with the Emperor on Denísov's behalf and get Denísov's petition handed in. When he and Borís were alone, Rostóv felt for the first time that he could not look Borís in the face without a sense of awkwardness. Borís, with one leg crossed over the other and stroking his left hand with the slender fingers of his right, listened to Rostóv as a general listens to the report of a subordinate, now looking aside and now gazing straight into Rostóv's eyes with the same veiled look. Each time this happened Rostóv felt uncomfortable and cast down his eyes.

"I have heard of such cases and know that His Majesty is very severe in such affairs. I think it would be best not to bring it before the Emperor, but to apply to the commander of the corps.... But in general, I think..."

"So you don't want to do anything? Well then, say so!" Rostóv almost shouted, not looking Borís in the face.

Borís smiled.

"On the contrary, I will do what I can. Only I thought..."

At that moment Zhilínski's voice was heard calling Borís.

"Well then, go, go, go..." said Rostóv, and refusing supper and remaining alone in the little room, he walked up and down for a long time, hearing the lighthearted French conversation from the next room.

CHAPTER XX

Rostóv had come to Tilsit the day least suitable for a petition on Denísov's behalf. He could not himself go to the general in attendance as he was in mufti and had come to Tilsit without permission to do so, and Borís, even had he wished to, could not have done so on the following day. On that day, June 27, the preliminaries of peace were signed. The Emperors exchanged decorations: Alexander received the Cross of the Legion of Honor and Napoleon the Order of St. Andrew of the First Degree, and a dinner had been arranged for the evening, given by a battalion of the French Guards to the Preobrazhénsk battalion. The Emperors were to be present at that banquet.

Rostóv felt so ill at ease and uncomfortable with Borís that, when the latter looked in after supper, he pretended to be asleep, and early next morning went away, avoiding Borís. In his civilian clothes and a round hat, he wandered about the town, staring at the French and their uniforms and at the streets and houses where the Russian and French Emperors were staying. In a square he saw tables being set up and preparations made for the dinner; he saw the Russian and French colors draped from side to side of the streets, with huge monograms *A* and *N*. In the windows of the houses also flags and bunting were displayed.

"Borís doesn't want to help me and I don't want to ask him. That's settled," thought Nicholas. "All is over between us, but I won't leave here without having done all I can for Denísov and certainly not without getting his letter to the Emperor. The Emperor!... He is here!" thought Rostóv, who had unconsciously returned to the house where Alexander lodged.

Saddled horses were standing before the house and the suite were assembling, evidently preparing for the Emperor to come out.

"I may see him at any moment," thought Rostóv. "If only I were to hand the letter direct to him and tell him all... could they really arrest me for my civilian clothes? Surely not! He would understand on whose side justice lies. He understands everything, knows everything. Who can be more just, more magnanimous than he? And even if they did arrest me for being here, what would it matter?" thought he, looking at an officer who was entering the house the Emperor occupied. "After all, people do go in.... It's all nonsense! I'll go in and hand the letter to the Emperor myself so much the worse for Drubetskóy who drives me to it!" And suddenly with a determination he himself did not expect, Rostóv felt for the letter in his pocket and went straight to the house.

"No, I won't miss my opportunity now, as I did after Austerlitz," he thought, expecting every moment to meet the monarch, and conscious of the blood that rushed to his heart at the thought. "I will fall at his feet and beseech him. He will lift me up, will listen, and will even thank me. 'I am happy when I can do good, but to remedy injustice is the greatest happiness,'" Rostóv fancied the sovereign saying. And passing people who looked after him with curiosity, he entered the porch of the Emperor's house.

A broad staircase led straight up from the entry, and to the right he saw a closed door. Below, under the staircase, was a door leading to the lower floor.

"Whom do you want?" someone inquired.

"To hand in a letter, a petition, to His Majesty," said Nicholas, with a tremor in his voice.

"A petition? This way, to the officer on duty" (he was shown the door leading downstairs), "only it won't be accepted."

On hearing this indifferent voice, Rostóv grew frightened at what he was doing; the thought of meeting the Emperor at any moment was so fascinating and consequently so alarming that he was ready to run away, but the official who had questioned him opened the door, and Rostóv entered.

A short stout man of about thirty, in white breeches and high boots and a batiste shirt that he had evidently only just put on, standing in that room, and his valet was buttoning on to the back of his breeches a new pair of handsome silk-embroidered braces that, for some reason, attracted Rostóv's attention. This man was speaking to someone in the adjoining room.

"A good figure and in her first bloom," he was saying, but on seeing Rostóv, he stopped short and frowned.

"What is it? A petition?"

"What is it?" asked the person in the other room.

"Another petitioner," answered the man with the braces.

"Tell him to come later. He'll be coming out directly, we must go."

"Later... later! Tomorrow. It's too late..."

Rostóv turned and was about to go, but the man in the braces stopped him.

"Whom have you come from? Who are you?"

"I come from Major Denísov," answered Rostóv.

"Are you an officer?"

"Lieutenant Count Rostóv."

"What audacity! Hand it in through your commander. And go along with you... go," and he continued to put on the uniform the valet handed him.

Rostóv went back into the hall and noticed that in the porch there were many officers and generals in full parade uniform, whom he had to pass.

Cursing his temerity, his heart sinking at the thought of finding himself at any moment face to face with the Emperor and being put to shame and arrested in his presence, fully alive now to the impropriety of his conduct and repenting of it, Rostóv, with downcast eyes, was making his way out of the house through the brilliant suite when a familiar voice called him and a hand detained him.

"What are you doing here, sir, in civilian dress?" asked a deep voice.

It was a cavalry general who had obtained the Emperor's special favor during this campaign, and who had formerly commanded the division in which Rostóv was serving.

Rostóv, in dismay, began justifying himself, but seeing the kindly, jocular face of the general, he took him aside and in an excited voice told him the whole affair, asking him to intercede for Denísov, whom the general knew. Having heard Rostóv to the end, the general shook his head gravely.

"I'm sorry, sorry for that fine fellow. Give me the letter."

Hardly had Rostóv handed him the letter and finished explaining Denísov's case, when hasty steps and the jingling of spurs were heard on the stairs, and the general, leaving him, went to the porch. The gentlemen of the Emperor's suite ran down the stairs and went to their horses. Hayne, the same groom who had been at Austerlitz, led up the Emperor's horse, and the faint creak of a footstep Rostóv knew at once was heard on the stairs. Forgetting the danger of being recognized, Rostóv went close to the porch, together with some inquisitive civilians, and again, after two years, saw those features he adored: that same face and same look and step, and the same union of majesty and mildness.... And the feeling of enthusiasm and love for his sovereign rose again in Rostóv's soul in all its old force. In the uniform of the Preobrazhénsk regiment—white chamois-leather breeches and high boots—and wearing a star Rostóv did not know (it was that of the *Légion d'honneur*), the monarch came out into the porch, putting on his gloves and carrying his hat under his arm. He stopped and looked about him, brightening everything around by his glance. He spoke a few words to some of the generals, and, recognizing the former commander of Rostóv's division, smiled and beckoned to him.

All the suite drew back and Rostóv saw the general talking for some time to the Emperor.

The Emperor said a few words to him and took a step toward his horse. Again the crowd of members of the suite and street gazers (among whom was Rostóv) moved nearer to the Emperor. Stopping beside his horse, with his hand on the saddle, the Emperor turned to the cavalry general and said in a loud voice, evidently wishing to be heard by all:

"I cannot do it, General. I cannot, because the law is stronger than I," and he raised his foot to the stirrup.

The general bowed his head respectfully, and the monarch mounted and rode down the street at a gallop. Beside himself with enthusiasm, Rostóv ran after him with the crowd.

CHAPTER XXI

The Emperor rode to the square where, facing one another, a battalion of the Preobrazhénsk regiment stood on the right and a battalion of the French Guards in their bearskin caps on the left.

As the Tsar rode up to one flank of the battalions, which presented arms, another group of horsemen galloped up to the opposite flank, and at the head of them Rostóv recognized Napoleon. It could be no one else. He came at a gallop, wearing a small hat, a blue uniform open over a white vest, and the St. Andrew ribbon over his shoulder. He was riding a very fine thoroughbred gray Arab horse with a crimson gold-embroidered saddlecloth. On approaching Alexander he raised his hat, and as he did so, Rostóv, with his cavalryman's eye, could not help noticing that Napoleon did not sit well or firmly in the saddle. The battalions shouted "Hurrah!" and *"Vivel'Empereur!"* Napoleon said something to Alexander, and both Emperors dismounted and took each other's hands. Napoleon's face wore an unpleasant and artificial smile. Alexander was saying something affable to him.

In spite of the trampling of the French gendarmes' horses, which were pushing back the crowd, Rostóv kept his eyes on every movement of Alexander and Bonaparte. It struck him as a surprise that Alexander treated Bonaparte as an equal and that the latter was quite at ease with the Tsar, as if such relations with an Emperor were an everyday matter to him.

Alexander and Napoleon, with the long train of their suites, approached the right flank of the Preobrazhénsk battalion and came straight up to the crowd standing there. The crowd unexpectedly found itself so close to the Emperors that Rostóv, standing in the front row, was afraid he might be recognized.

"Sire, I ask your permission to present the Legion of Honor to the bravest of your soldiers," said a sharp, precise voice, articulating every letter.

This was said by the undersized Napoleon, looking up straight into Alexander's eyes. Alexander listened attentively to what was said to him and, bending his head, smiled pleasantly.

"To him who has borne himself most bravely in this last war," added Napoleon, accentuating each syllable, as with a composure and assurance exasperating to Rostóv, he ran his eyes over the Russian ranks drawn up before him, who all presented arms with their eyes fixed on their Emperor.

"Will Your Majesty allow me to consult the colonel?" said Alexander and took a few hasty steps toward Prince Kozlóvski, the commander of the battalion.

Bonaparte meanwhile began taking the glove off his small white hand, tore it in doing so, and threw it away. An aide-de-camp behind him rushed forward and picked it up.

"To whom shall it be given?" the Emperor Alexander asked Kozlóvski, in Russian in a low voice.

"To whomever Your Majesty commands."

The Emperor knit his brows with dissatisfaction and, glancing back, remarked:

"But we must give him an answer."

Kozlóvski scanned the ranks resolutely and included Rostóv in his scrutiny.

"Can it be me?" thought Rostóv.

"Lázarev!" the colonel called, with a frown, and Lázarev, the first soldier in the rank, stepped briskly forward.

"Where are you off to? Stop here!" voices whispered to Lázarev who did not know where to go. Lázarev stopped, casting a sidelong look at his colonel in alarm. His face twitched, as often happens to soldiers called before the ranks.

Napoleon slightly turned his head, and put his plump little hand out behind him as if to take something. The members of his suite, guessing at once what he wanted, moved about and whispered as they passed something from one to another, and a page—the same one Rostóv had seen the previous evening at Borís'—ran forward and, bowing respectfully over the outstretched hand and not keeping it waiting a moment, laid in it an Order on a red ribbon. Napoleon, without looking, pressed two fingers together and the badge was between them. Then he approached Lázarev (who rolled his eyes and persistently gazed at his own monarch), looked round at the Emperor Alexander to imply that what he was now doing was done for the sake of his ally, and the small white hand holding the Order touched one of Lázarev's buttons. It was as if Napoleon knew that it was only necessary for his hand to deign to touch that soldier's breast for the soldier to be forever happy, rewarded, and distinguished from everyone else in the world. Napoleon merely laid the cross on Lázarev's breast and, dropping his hand, turned toward Alexander as though sure that the cross would adhere there. And it really did.

Officious hands, Russian and French, immediately seized the cross and fastened it to the uniform. Lázarev glanced morosely at the little man with white hands who was doing something to him and, still standing motionless presenting arms, looked again straight into Alexander's eyes, as if asking whether he should stand there, or go away, or do something else. But receiving no orders, he remained for some time in that rigid position.

The Emperors remounted and rode away. The Preobrazhénsk battalion, breaking rank, mingled with the French Guards and sat down at the tables prepared for them.

Lázarev sat in the place of honor. Russian and French officers embraced him, congratulated him, and pressed his hands. Crowds of officers and civilians drew near merely to see him. A rumble of Russian and French voices and laughter filled the air round the tables in the square. Two officers with flushed faces, looking cheerful and happy, passed by Rostóv.

"What d'you think of the treat? All on silver plate," one of them was saying. "Have you seen Lázarev?"

"I have."

"Tomorrow, I hear, the Preobrazhénskis will give them a dinner."

"Yes, but what luck for Lázarev! Twelve hundred francs' pension for life."

"Here's a cap, lads!" shouted a Preobrazhénsk soldier, donning a shaggy French cap.

"It's a fine thing! First-rate!"

"Have you heard the password?" asked one Guards' officer of another. "The day before yesterday it was '*Napoléon, France, bravoure*'; yesterday, '*Alexandre, Russie, grandeur.*' One day our Emperor gives it and next day Napoleon. Tomorrow our Emperor will send a St. George's Cross to the bravest of the French Guards. It has to be done. He must respond in kind."

Borís, too, with his friend Zhilínski, came to see the Preobrazhénsk banquet. On his way back, he noticed Rostóv standing by the corner of a house.

"Rostóv! How d'you do? We missed one another," he said, and could not refrain from asking what was the matter, so strangely dismal and troubled was Rostóv's face.

"Nothing, nothing," replied Rostóv.

"You'll call round?"

"Yes, I will."

Rostóv stood at that corner for a long time, watching the feast from a distance. In his mind, a painful process was going on which he could not bring to a conclusion. Terrible doubts rose in his soul. Now he remembered Denísov with his changed expression, his submission, and the whole hospital, with arms and legs torn off and its dirt and disease. So vividly did he recall that hospital stench of dead flesh that he looked round to see where the smell came from. Next he thought of that self-satisfied Bonaparte, with his small white hand, who was now an Emperor, liked and respected by Alexander. Then why those severed arms and legs and those dead men?... Then again he thought of Lázarev rewarded and Denísov punished and unpardoned. He caught himself harboring such strange thoughts that he was frightened.

The smell of the food the Preobrazhénskis were eating and a sense of hunger recalled him from these reflections; he had to get something to eat before going away. He went to a hotel he had noticed that morning. There he found so many people, among them officers who, like himself, had come in civilian clothes, that he had difficulty in getting a dinner. Two officers of his own division joined him. The conversation naturally turned on the peace. The officers, his comrades, like most of the army, were dissatisfied with the peace concluded after the battle of Friedland. They said that had we held out a little longer Napoleon would have been done for, as his troops had neither provisions nor ammunition. Nicholas ate and drank (chiefly the latter) in silence. He finished a couple of bottles of wine by himself. The process in his mind went on tormenting him without reaching a conclusion. He feared to give way to his thoughts, yet could not get rid of them. Suddenly, on one of the officers' saying that it was humiliating to look at the French, Rostóv began shouting with uncalled-for wrath, and therefore much to the surprise of the officers:

"How can you judge what's best?" he cried, the blood suddenly rushing to his face. "How can you judge the Emperor's actions? What right have we to argue? We cannot comprehend either the Emperor's aims or his actions!"

"But I never said a word about the Emperor!" said the officer, justifying himself, and unable to understand Rostóv's outburst, except on the supposition that he was drunk.

But Rostóv did not listen to him.

"We are not diplomatic officials, we are soldiers and nothing more," he went on. "If we are ordered to die, we must die. If we're punished, it means that we have deserved it, it's not for us to judge. If the Emperor pleases to recognize Bonaparte as Emperor and to conclude an alliance with him, it means that that is the right thing to do. If once we begin judging and arguing about everything, nothing sacred will be left! That way we shall be saying there is no God— nothing!" shouted Nicholas, banging the table—very little to the point as it seemed to his listeners, but quite relevantly to the course of his own thoughts.

"Our business is to do our duty, to fight and not to think! That's all...." said he.

"And to drink," said one of the officers, not wishing to quarrel.

"Yes, and to drink," assented Nicholas. "Hullo there! Another bottle!" he shouted.

In 1808 the Emperor Alexander went to Erfurt for a fresh interview with the Emperor Napoleon, and in the upper circles of Petersburg there was much talk of the grandeur of this important meeting.

CHAPTER XXII

In 1809 the intimacy between "the world's two arbiters," as Napoleon and Alexander were called, was such that when Napoleon declared war on Austria a Russian corps crossed the frontier to co-operate with our old enemy Bonaparte against our old ally the Emperor of Austria, and in court circles the possibility of marriage between Napoleon and one of Alexander's sisters was spoken of. But besides considerations of foreign policy, the attention of Russian society was at that time keenly directed on the internal changes that were being undertaken in all the departments of government.

Life meanwhile—real life, with its essential interests of health and sickness, toil and rest, and its intellectual interests in thought, science, poetry, music, love, friendship, hatred, and passions—went on as usual, independently of and apart from political friendship or enmity with Napoleon Bonaparte and from all the schemes of reconstruction.